Love hates the game of words...

Lauren Wilt—Her star falling, this award-winning but aging novelist rejuvenates her career by writing a successful singles column. Too bad it couldn't do the same for her figure. With her fortunes skyrocketing, she needed a pretty face to live up to public expectations.

Helen Matter—Young. Attractive. Blond. Blue-eyed. Extremely intelligent. Fashion disaster. Dating train wreck. Every man's dream just wasn't being advertised properly. Until *she* became the face of Chicago's hottest news topic: "The Single Life."

Enter: gentleman callers, inquisitive media and mutually assured disaster.

Is there a lesson to be learned in loving the single life?

Liz Wood

Liz Wood has lived on four different continents and in twice as many countries, but her favorite things remain quite domestic: books, chocolate and coffee, preferably all together. She reads everything from French comics to Italian scandal sheets, German philosophy to American romances (the latter late into the night). When she is not reading, she is trying to train her beagle to do some housekeeping, so she can have more time to, um, read.

THE SINGLE LIFE

LIZ WOOD

THE SINGLE LIFE

copyright © 2006 by Liz Wood

i s b n 0 3 7 3 8 8 0 8 9 8

TheNextNovel.com

 HARLEQUIN®

PRINTED IN U.S.A.

From the Author

Dear Reader,

The idea for *The Single Life* came to me one afternoon when a friend and her seventy-something mother described the latter's recent experiences with Internet dating. As we laughed about the complicated security measures they had adopted to protect her from senile Don Juans and toothless Lotharios, I began to wonder what insights she might bring to a singles column. Were her experiences all that different from younger women who keep looking for a crock of good men at the end of the rocky road to romance?

I'm still not entirely sure about the answer to that question, but I did realize something else that afternoon: it's never too late to begin again. This realization guided me as I sketched out the story of the unlikely friendship between three women trying to turn their lives around. Though they face very different challenges in their single lives, fifty-something Lauren, forty-something Clare and twenty-something Helen come away with the same lesson: the immeasurable value of friendship.

I hope you will have as much pleasure reading about these singles as I had writing about them.

Liz

Many thanks to Tara Gavin, whose suggestions for
revision went right to the heart of the matter. Thanks
also to Lena Wood for being such a generous guinea pig.

I dedicate this book to my mother who, despite her many
experiences, has never really known the single life.

CHAPTER 1

Borrow my words, then!—
Your beautiful young manhood—lend me that!
And we two make one hero of romance!

        Edmond Rostand, Cyrano de Bergerac

"You're going to have to sell the house."

Lauren shut her eyes tightly, hoping that she hadn't heard correctly, that she was still asleep and would wake up to something other than the jarring sound of the telephone and Clare's devastating proclamation. After all those hours spent exploring the varied shades of darkness, she wasn't even sure she had actually slept. Not until she heard Clare Hanley's voice at the other end of the line.

"What time is it anyway?" she asked in a hoarse voice.

"Way past the time for you to be still in bed. The last time I looked, it was going on eleven. What happened? Did you stay up to catch the late show?"

"Something like that."

Lauren didn't want to go into the details of her sleepless nights.

"Well, I'm sorry if I've ruined your beauty sleep, but I'm glad you finally answered. I've been trying to reach you for days. Don't you ever listen to your messages?"

"I listen to them." She just didn't bother to answer them. These days she also didn't bother to answer the phone. She wouldn't have picked up this time, either, except that Chrissie had said she would call, and Lauren really wanted to speak to her, to hear her voice, to know she was all right.

E-mail could get the news through. It could transmit a quick greeting or forward a funny joke, but it couldn't reassure Lauren about the subtleties, the unspoken nuances that Chrissie couldn't hide from her mother.

They had been playing telephone tag for days now. Neither Lauren's preference for the answering machine, nor the time difference between Illinois and Vienna helped much. So when the phone had rung at 11:00 a.m., Lauren had quickly calculated that it was late afternoon for Chrissie in Austria and a perfect time for a trans-Atlantic conversation. She had wiped her eyes and swallowed the big lump in her throat. By the time the phone had rung a third time, she was rolling across the king-size bed and reaching for the receiver. She didn't stop to think it might be someone other than Chrissie.

Now here she was, stuck with the effects of another bad

night's sleep, a headache that was getting worse by the second and a conversation she really didn't want to have.

"As you can probably tell, I just woke up, Clare, and this is really a bad time to talk. I'll call you back. Bye—"

"Don't you dare hang up on me, Lauren Wilt! I've waited long enough to speak to you, and I'm not going through this again."

Lauren didn't say anything, but she didn't hang up either. Even outside the courtroom, Clare's voice could put fear in humble citizens like herself.

Clare must have realized it because she switched to a softer tone.

"How've you been, Lauren?"

"Fine, Clare. Just fine. As long as people don't try to get me out of bed before twelve."

"Mmm-hmm. That's why you haven't been answering your phone lately? Or responding to your messages?"

"I've been, you know, busy."

"Yeah, so have I. But I return my calls."

"You pay other people to do it for you."

"Same thing. Besides, I'm not just talking about business calls. Even your best friend Alice says you haven't been returning her calls either."

"I was going to today. I've been trying to finish a chapter." Trying being the operative word, since Lauren hadn't managed to finish it. She had spent another day looking at a blank screen—when she wasn't contemplating her blank mind. She didn't expect today would be much different. Which was why she hadn't bothered to get out of bed, even when it was clear she wasn't going to get back to sleep.

"Look, Lauren, I'm your lawyer, but I'm speaking here as your friend. It's been more than a year since the divorce came through. You need to start living again."

It was easy for Clare to talk. She'd never been divorced. Never been married, for that matter. Never had her heart broken. Never had to mend it. Not independent, hard-as-nails Clare Hanley.

"Is that why you called? To offer me some friendly advice? For free?"

"Actually, no. I just gave you the free advice, but I called about something else. And that, as you know, doesn't come free. You pay for it. So, like it or not, I have to give it to you."

Clare paused for a moment, as if she were weighing her words. When she spoke again, she sounded surprisingly unsure of herself. "Lauren, I think you should come in so we can talk about it."

"If it's so important, you should tell me over the phone."

"Lauren, look, maybe we could meet for lunch or dinner—my treat, of course—and we can talk about this."

"I already have plans for lunch."

Not! As Chrissie might say. The old Lauren would have crossed her fingers because she was telling a lie. But the new Lauren—who was really a very old Lauren—a very, very old, tired, worn-out Lauren—didn't bother with that. She just didn't see the point anymore, no more than having lunch with Clare, or anyone else for that matter.

"With Alice?" Clare was asking. "That's okay. She can come, too."

"No, not with Alice."

"Lauren—"

"Just tell me, Clare. I may not be a courtroom shark like you, but I'm no hothouse flower either."

"I just think you'd be better off dealing with this face-to-face."

"Just tell me."

"Okay." Clare sighed. "If that's the way you want it."

Lauren didn't say anything, but her silence was eloquent. After a moment, Clare spoke.

"I've been looking into your accounts and, well, I don't think you're going to be able to keep up with all your payments. There's no two ways about this—you're going to have to sell the house."

Lauren's first reaction was to think she hadn't heard correctly. Her second was much more passionate.

"Sell the house? Are you crazy? Never!"

"Lauren, listen to me. I know what it means to you. I know it was once your grandmother's house. I know how important it is to you, how much you want to keep it. You made it very clear when we were working on the divorce settlement. You gave up a lot for it—against my better advice, I might add."

"You're off the hook."

"Honestly, Lauren! That's the *least* of my worries."

"So what are your worries?" Other than trying to keep Lauren on the phone as long as possible when all she wanted to do was hang up and have another cry.

"Mostly that you're not in the same position you were. You lost money on your investments, and now with the increases in property tax, well, I just don't see how you can make your payments."

Lauren pressed her fingers against her forehead in the hopes of quelling the ache that was increasing by the minute.

"I'll cut down on the rest of my spending if I have to, but I can't sell the house."

"It's going to take a lot more than better budgeting. You just don't have the income anymore."

"What about the money my mother left me?"

"We put it in trust for Chrissie and Jeff. Against my—"

"Better advice, I know. You're beginning to repeat yourself. Couldn't we get an extension on the taxes? Negotiate somehow?"

"With what? It's not as if you have a new source of revenue. You're already living on the advance for your next book—which you aren't even close to delivering—not even now that the deadline has come and gone. And from what you've been telling me, there's nothing else in the pipeline."

"There must be something we can do! Help me out here, Clare. Please." Lauren could hear her voice breaking, but she didn't try to hold back. She couldn't, even if she wanted to.

"I'm sorry, Lauren. Really, I am. I've looked at it from all angles and there's nothing I can do. Unless you come up with more money soon, my only suggestion is to sell the house. Because even if you have your miracle, even if you get more money, you're still not in the clear. An old house like yours, the repairs are endless. The bills won't stop. They'll just keep coming. They'll soak up all your money and then some. Listen to me, Lauren. Sell the house."

Clare slammed the phone down, more annoyed with herself than with Lauren. After more than twenty years in the business, she should be more tactful, more considerate, more kind when dealing with the financial and legal affairs of a woman whose heart had been ripped in two and whose life was broken—especially when the woman was also a friend.

But Clare had never been very good at holding hands and passing the Kleenex. Maybe because she'd had her own share of hard luck—and then some— when most kids were still wiping their eyes over Bambi's mother and Simba's father. Maybe because she'd learned early that no amount of hand-holding and Kleenex-wringing would pay the bills. Only hard cash would, aided by calculating law. That's where she came in. The rest would take time—a lot of time.

But time was something Lauren didn't have, at least not when it came to the house. Not that Clare thought Lauren should hang on to the house. Even with the crippling bills, Lauren was holding on to it harder than any life belt, as if it were the only thing keeping her alive now that her husband, her children and her creative inspiration were gone. Clare knew there were days, weeks even, when Lauren didn't leave her cocoon. But that didn't change the fact that no house—not even a gingerbread one with gaily painted walls, shining wooden floors, tower bedrooms and shingled turrets— could put Lauren's life back together. Only Lauren could do that.

Still, Clare wished there were something she could do. There must be something she'd missed when she'd explored all the angles with her long-time colleague, the top-notch financial planner Lynne Pozzorni. Lynne had been disappointed with some of the choices Lauren had made and hadn't hidden it from Clare.

"We women never learn, do we?" she had said, shaking her head in dismay and disapproval. "We want to be nice and kind and generous. We forget it's a world of wolves out there—and our exes are the meanest and the cruelest. We must be genetically programmed for it. That's the only way I can explain it."

Clare wasn't sure genetics had anything to do with it, but she knew what Lynne meant. She had seen it often enough with other cases. Divorcing mothers ready to forego everything but regular child support payments—only to learn that no provisions had been made for hefty college tuition fees down the line. Middle-aged women who gave up their life savings to pay off their new spouse's debts—only to lose that investment and much more when the rosy first blush of the honeymoon disappeared into the darkness of a divorce settlement. Good-hearted women who trusted their husbands with managing their incomes—only to discover the man had been stashing cash and hiding assets.

Small wonder Clare had never bothered to tie a knot. When office gossips speculated about her, they agreed on one point: Clare was a cold-hearted cynic who would never give happily ever after and true love a chance. They were not wrong. It was hard not to be a cold-hearted cynic when you knew what cruelty, insincerity and selfishness lie in the hearts of men. And as attentive as she was to using gender-neutral terms, Clare really did have the male of the species in mind.

Office gossip didn't know there was a time when Clare hadn't thought that way. When she had been wrapped in the soft tissue of romantic love. When she had believed it was the magic cloak that would keep all evil, pain and heartache away.

That had been a long time ago, a lifetime. Which was why it was hard to understand why her throat was constricted now, her chest tight, her eyes watery. Whatever would the office gossips say if they knew?

Clare forced herself to swallow. She was overreacting to Lauren's call. She was letting her friend's situation get to her. She was trying to do the hand-holding and the Kleenex-wringing when she was better off leaving that to someone else. Someone like Alice. She would call Lauren's oldest and closest friend and see what the two of them could do.

Or rather what Alice could do because Clare could only continue doing what she had been doing for the last twenty years. What she was paid to do. What had got her here, in the corner office with a view of Lake Michigan, a personal assistant on call, a BMW in the garage, a wardrobe that would make an upcoming starlet envious, and more than her share of fun—nights of fun, weekends of fun, a lot of money's worth of fun.

But no one to go home to.

It's bad enough to arrive home one night to discover your housemate naked on the living room couch. It's worse, when someone else is with her, as naked as she is. Worst of all is recognizing the naked guy is someone you introduced her to, someone who you thought might get naked with you.

Not that Helen Matter really, truly wanted to get naked with Josh. He was just another techno-weenie who cared more about bytes and transfer protocols than romantic, candlelit dinners—a dandruff-coated techno-weenie in the familiar uniform of jeans, white socks and an oversized, long-sleeve shirt.

On a scale of one to ten, he was probably a two, or a one and a half. But scales were for women who could choose between Matt Damon and Matt LeBlanc, Jude Law and Justin Timberlake. Not for a woman who had to choose between Josh and nothing. Until she had walked in the door the other night, she had thought at least *that* choice was hers.

Helen had known Josh as a fellow graduate student for some time, but hadn't thought twice about him. Which was surprising given how these days she thought a lot about guys and a lot more about why she didn't have one in her life.

So she had been happy when she and Josh had managed to find something to talk about other than techno-jargon. The lab computer had crashed one evening while they were testing a new program, and he had filled in the silence with an account of his bicycle trip in Germany, which had been more fun than the year before when he had interned at his step-father's firm, and he especially enjoyed it because of the model of bike he was riding, which he preferred to the sixteen-speeder he'd had as an undergrad. She had tried to look interested, although she was really almost numb with boredom. Even so, when he had suggested they go to the movies afterward, she had agreed.

This is it, she had thought. This is the start of something new, wild and passionate! He will be Paris to my Helen, Lord Devlin to my Althea, Rhett to my Scarlett.

Now, she couldn't even remember what movie they saw, only that it had something to do with robots taking over the world. Not exactly what she considered a great choice for a first date. Because even though they had bought their own tickets, hadn't shared popcorn or even come close to holding hands, she considered the outing a date.

When the film was over, they had gone to her house. He'd met Sharon then and all three of them had gone out again to the neighborhood bar. Helen hadn't seen Josh much after that. Duh! He was at her place with Sharon while Helen was at the lab alone.

Just as well. Josh was really not what she was looking for. If Sharon wanted him, she could have him. As long as it wasn't on Helen's couch and in her living room.

And if Sharon got everything she wanted from Josh on the nights of his visits, she didn't get an easy response from Helen.

"What's the big deal?" she had asked, when Helen

broached the subject. "It's not as if he is, like, your boyfriend."

"You were doing it on the couch, Sharon, in the living room."

"So?"

"So? Something called privacy—your space, my space, our space." Helen flapped her hands at the designated spaces, but the gesturing didn't help. Sharon just stared back at her, uncomprehending.

"Whatever!" She rolled her eyes and held both palms out to show that the discussion was over. "If you're not happy, you can, like, find someplace else to go."

Which was what Helen was going to do, even though the lease was in her name. If anyone should leave, it should be Sharon, who was only supposed to be in Chrissie Wilt Gard's room for a short while, anyway.

"I'm not really moving out," Chrissie had said more than a year ago, "so don't look for another roomie. I love my mother, but I can't live with her too long. She'd drive me crazy."

Helen didn't know how mothers could do that because she had been only eight when hers had died. But Chrissie usually knew what she was talking about. Only it hadn't been Chrissie who had been going crazy. It had been her mother. Not crazy, really. Just heartbroken.

So, despite her reservations, Chrissie had moved to her mother's Oak Park house, where she had remained for more than a year. Then, she had been offered her dream job in Austria as the legal advisor to an international trade organization. Even then, she hadn't wanted to leave.

"I can't leave my mom. Not now. Not when she's like this."

"She wants you to go, Chrissie," Helen had reminded her. "And you can't turn down something like this. You've wanted it, like, forever."

Chrissie had shrugged her shoulders, but in the end she had gone. Now Helen was also going to have to go. She didn't want Sharon thinking she begrudged her Josh.

Because she really didn't care about him. In fact, the more she thought about it, the less she cared. Sure, it had surprised her to see them together. Maybe even shocked her that Josh, just another techno-weenie, could do it in the living room, with the door wide open. Maybe even amazed her that he could get her roommate to make such loud noises.

But neither the sight nor the sounds really bothered her. What really bothered her was that she hadn't even been good enough for a techno-weenie.

Well, she was going to change all that. She would deal with her lack-of-man problem the way she had dealt with all her problems. The way she had managed to outsmart her brother David at chess and her other brother Christopher at the International Youth for Robotics Fair. The way she had managed to get top marks in graduate school. All she had to do was find the right books, take the right classes, read, study and then master the subject. It couldn't be that difficult, could it?

But first, she was going to have to find another place to live.

CHAPTER 2

Lauren pushed the diced carrots around her plate. Alice Mirosek was saying something about her husband Frank and his camera. Or was it his carburetor? Did it really matter? Either way, Lauren had lost the point to the story, and no one seemed to notice. Why had she come? Why had she let Alice and Clare talk her into it?

Not that there had been any discussion involved. They had pulled the good cop/bad cop routine. First, the good cop had called about the planned get-together.

"I never get to see you anymore now that the kids are gone and you've stopped coming to the fitness classes," Alice had said in that honeyed voice of hers. "It would be nice to catch up. Let's try lunch at The Green Factory. Clare can make it, too. It'll be fun, Lauren. Just like old times."

But it wouldn't be like old times, not for her anyway. Those times were gone. Gone with the wind. Make that the hurricane.

So Lauren hadn't promised anything, and she certainly hadn't bothered to get ready for lunch today. But she hadn't figured on the bad cop arriving. Like a dark-haired Valkyrie in pursuit of revenge, Clare had pushed her straight into the shower, thrown some clothes on her bed and practically forced her into the car. Nor did her relentless takeover stop when they arrived at The Green Factory. She wouldn't even allow Lauren to give her order to the boyish-looking waiter. Not that it mattered. She didn't care what it was anyway, even though she had had a mouthful or two.

Lauren glanced at her friends. At least, they weren't having any trouble eating. No more than they were with life. No road blocks on their paths to happiness, not even a bump.

Clare said something indiscernible. Alice nodded and continued to talk about Frank. That marriage was obviously still going strong. Which was somewhat surprising, given all the odds against them.

Frank, the rebellious son of New Jersey factory workers, had traded in his youthful rock musician aspirations to work with emotionally disturbed children. Alice was born and bred in the affluent suburb of Oak Park, and it showed, right down to her woolen knit skirt, sensible but expensive leather shoes, and her senior management position at a Chicago bank. Yet Frank and Alice had found something together that Charles and Lauren, with their similar backgrounds, never had. Now that Frank and Alice's youngest was almost out of college, it seemed to be honeymoon time all over again for them. No wonder Alice couldn't understand what Lauren was going through. No more than Clare could.

Lauren turned toward the other woman whose black hair, olive-toned skin and dark eyes revealed her Mediterranean origins. She was saying something in her eloquent, persuasive style, gesturing in short, rapid movements to hammer home a point. Lauren noticed again how tiny Clare's wrists were, making her seem fragile and delicate.

But there was nothing delicate or fragile about Clare. Lauren knew that for a fact. Clare clearly didn't need anything or anyone—not a husband, not children. Lauren had always thought how empty Clare's days must be without them. But, looking at her now, it was clear that Clare's life could hardly be qualified a failure.

Unlike Lauren's.

Suddenly aware of a lull in the conversation and two pairs of eyes scrutinizing her, Lauren impaled something on her fork and dragged it into her mouth. She chewed with effort, and the big, tasteless lump went down slowly, very slowly.

She didn't notice Alice reaching over until she felt the squeeze of her hand.

"Clare told me about the house," Alice said, slowly releasing her grip. "I'm sorry."

Tilting her head, letting her shoulder-length hair

fall around her face like a veil, Lauren kept her eyes on her plate. "Yeah, well."

"Three heads are better than one, you know. Together we'll think of something."

"Have *you* thought about it?" Clare asked. "What you're going to do with it?"

Lauren lifted her head. "I don't know. I really don't. I just know I can't sell it. Not after all the time I put into it. Not now that I've lost everything else. The house…" She glanced around the restaurant and swallowed, hoping no one noticed the break in her voice. She forced herself to look back at the two women. "That would be the last straw."

"You haven't lost everything, Lauren," Alice said. "You have to stop thinking that way."

"Right." Lauren set her fork on her plate and leaned back in her chair. "And which way should I be thinking?"

"Certainly not only about the bad things. Think about the good things. You have two wonderful children, a house you restored practically on your own, an award-winning book. Should I continue?"

Lauren shrugged. "What's the point?" She studied the pattern on the table cloth, hoping the conversation would change and her friends would ignore her, the way the rest of the universe had been doing. But she underestimated them.

"Oh for crying out loud, Lauren!" Clare said, running her manicured fingers through her dark curls. "You've got to stop thinking this way. The world hasn't ended just because you lost your husband! Maybe you didn't lose anything. Maybe you just got rid of something old and useless. Maybe this is your chance to begin something new."

"Clare, I'm fifty-three," Lauren retorted. "You don't begin something at fifty-three. You begin to end it. Unless you're me, and it's already over." She smiled brightly at her weak attempt at humor.

Clare didn't respond in kind. Her features seemed sterner, and she shook her head emphatically. "It's not over. Not all of it, anyway. It's time for you to say goodbye to one part of your life and move on to the next." She blew out slowly, then continued in a more restrained tone. "I mean, it's not as if we just have a single shot at doing something with our lives."

Alice nodded. "Or one way of living it."

"I can't. I'm just not cut out for any other kind of life. I really don't think I can manage this...this...this single life." Lauren pointed at the air, as if to provide a clearer idea of what she was talking about.

"You don't know that until you've tried," Alice said. "Things change, and we keep on living."

"That's easy for you to say. You still have your life, the one you've always had, the one you've always wanted."

"Not exactly."

Alice sounded almost wistful, but Lauren knew that wasn't possible. She was projecting her own failures and disappointments onto her friend. Alice really did have everything—a career on track, a husband who obviously loved her more than ever and two children, living close enough to visit, whose only contact didn't have to be through the telephone or the Internet.

"You think your life is over when you could be entering one of the most exciting periods," Alice continued. "Just think of all the exciting, new places you could visit, the fun things you could do, the great guys you could meet."

"Men are not interested in me." Lauren waved her hands over her chest, where, even with a firm underwire bra, her breasts sagged. She didn't need to point at the rest of her. She was obviously a dismal heap.

"You don't know that," Clare said. "You haven't bothered to get in touch with that writer who your agent Louise has been trying to set you up with."

"Or that guy who Chrissie has been wanting you to meet," Alice added. "She certainly thinks someone might be interested in you."

"Chrissie's just being a good daughter," Lauren replied. "Nothing can shake her faith in me."

"So learn from her and stop feeling sorry for yourself. Your life isn't over. It's just beginning. Think of it as…as…as…" Alice's face suddenly brightened. "I know, as the dawning of a new age."

Alice must be listening to Frank's old albums, Lauren thought, bemused. She wanted to remind her friend how outdated that kind of talk was. But Alice seemed so sincere, Lauren didn't have the heart. Besides, she suddenly realized how hard Clare and Alice were trying, for her sake. Surely, the least she could do was listen.

"Go ahead," she said, forcing herself to smile at the concerned faces. "Explain."

"It's just a question of changing your attitude. Your husband walked out? Good riddance," Alice said.

"That's what I would say. *What* I say." Clare nodded approvingly. "I mean, come on Lauren, think of what Charles did to you. It's not as if he was ever really there for you. You know that."

Alice leaned forward. "Besides, now you don't have to waste your time socializing with his colleagues at those silly dinner parties you hated."

This time, Lauren's smile was genuine. "I did hate them."

Charles had always argued that part of his career depended on pleasing the people he worked with. So Lauren had accepted the role of hostess, even when it hadn't been what she wanted. She certainly didn't miss that part of her former life!

"See what I mean?" Alice said. She tilted her head slightly. With her mousy curls framing her face, she suddenly looked cherubic, despite her fifty-something years.

"Maybe." Lauren shrugged her shoulders. "But that's just one thing. What about everything else?"

Clare opened her mouth, then closed it to smile at the waiter, returning to check on them. Alice asked for more bread.

"About Charles…" Clare began when the waiter left.

"No, forget about him." Lauren waved her hands. "He wouldn't matter so much if I could finish this book. What about not being able to write? That has *never* happened to me. *Never*. Not even when Chrissie was a baby, and Jeff was three, and between the two of them, I was up all night and all day. I was exhausted, but I wrote. Nothing memorable, of course, but I wrote. I can't even do that now."

The two women exchanged glances. Clare shrugged, and Alice spoke.

"Maybe you're writing about the wrong thing. When the kids were small, what did you write about?"

"Them. Me. Parenting. Our lives. Stuff like that. Like I said, most of it was pretty bad, but it gave me a routine that I could stick to. Now, I can't think of a paragraph, a sentence, a word to put down."

Alice smiled sympathetically. "I understand. But the book you won the award for was about the house, your family, the people and things you love, right?"

"*Autobiography of a House?* Yes, you could say that." Lauren narrowed her eyes, realizing where Alice was going. "But my current project, *My Mother's Garden*, is about the same sort of thing. Only this time, I just can't write. So there goes your theory."

"Maybe you've said all you have to say about it," Alice continued. "Start thinking about something else and maybe you'll begin to write again."

"That would be great if it weren't for a little thing called a contract," Lauren said.

Alice looked at Clare for help.

"Be inventive. Your editor has agreed to extend the deadline, hasn't she?" Clare began, then paused as the waiter arrived with the bread and waited for him to leave. "Like I was saying, maybe you can persuade your editor that this other topic—the one you are going to come up with—is really great. Talk to your agent. Talk to Louise. That's what she's there for."

"You make it sound so easy, Clare. It's not."

"I never said it was." Clare's hands thumped lightly against the tabletop. "I just said you have to think about things differently. It's a start."

"Maybe." Lauren picked up her fork again and pushed it around her plate, shaping the untouched food into a mound. "But here's the real test. What do I do about the house?"

Alice looked at Lauren's plate. "Have some bread. It's whole wheat, the kind you like. Go ahead. Dip it in the yogurt sauce."

Alice did just that, but Lauren didn't follow suit. Instead she watched, enjoying Alice's obvious pleasure in the food, despite her own dark mood.

"Go on, Lauren. Have some." Clare helped herself to

some bread and dipped it in the sauce. "We don't want you missing out on a good thing. That's what you said to me the first time you brought me here. Remember?"

Lauren remembered. She and Alice had been rewarding themselves here regularly with good, healthy food after grueling sessions at the fitness class. When they had befriended Clare, a sister in sweat, they had invited her along. But the vegetarian menu didn't thrill Clare. The first couple of times she'd ordered only salads. She even joked about it: the Green Factory became the Slim Factory and the name stuck for a while.

Then, one day, Clare became adventurous. She tried a tofu burger and liked it. The next time, she moved on to the lentil loaf. After that, it was the olive-roasted bread, millet pilaf and vegetable croustade. Now, she was a jolly green monster, insisting Lauren eat bread. Everyone else worried about carbs, but Clare pushed bread!

Lauren forced herself to eat some in a show of good will. For some reason, it took less effort to get it down than whatever had been on her plate.

"Happy?" She looked at Alice who was leaning back, her hands folded across her stomach. "Aren't you going to have any more?"

Alice shook her head. "I've had too much already. Not that I can stop myself. I'm addicted. I've got the hips to show for it."

She patted them, inviting Lauren to look at the parts of her figure visible behind the table. It was full and ample and curvaceous. Lauren wished she looked half as healthy and a quarter as feminine.

"You don't have anything to worry about. Besides, I think it's going to happen, addiction or not. It has something to do with meno... No, what did you call it? Oh, yes. The dawn of a new age. You don't loose your figure, you just gain a middle."

Alice wagged her finger. "Careful, Lauren. I'm going to think you agree with me."

"Help me with my house and I just might."

Clare became suddenly serious. "Look, as your lawyer, I really think your best option is to sell."

"I told you—" Lauren began, but closed her mouth when Clare lifted up a dainty index finger.

"Alice and I have been talking about it, and we think, well, there is something you could try."

"What?" Lauren reached for some water.

"Get a job."

Lauren almost knocked her glass down. "A job? I have one. It's called writing."

"And apparently, it's not going too well."

Once again, Lauren opened her mouth to say something; once again, Clare persevered.

"I'm talking about another job, Lauren. One that would get you some cash. And it would have other advantages. It would get you out of the house. It could give you something to write about." She held up three fingers. "It might even shake your depression."

Clare dropped her hand, leaned her elbows on the table and moved closer to Lauren. "I'm serious, Lauren. Get a job, and you just might be set for that new life we were talking about."

"Get a job?" Lauren looked at Alice for help and saw that the battle lines had been drawn earlier, probably before she had arrived at the table. "I wouldn't know how to do that. The last time I tried was a lifetime ago. And who's going to want a woman who's over the hill, anyway?"

"Well, if that's the way you think, no one!" Alice said, impatience straining her voice for the first time. "Shake out of it, honey. You may not be the only one who's got problems around here, but you're the only one who's determined not to do something about them!"

Lauren was so startled by the uncharacteristic outburst, she stopped listening until Clare pounded her fist against the table.

"You really haven't been hearing a word we've been saying, have you? Well listen to this. It's all about attitude. Convince yourself and you'll convince others."

Chrissie hadn't needed any convincing. She had been delighted with Clare's and Alice's idea and had urged her mother to explore the professional contacts she had developed over the years. Western University, where Lauren had taught years ago, might have short-term jobs. With the semester beginning soon and the increase in enrolments, the school would be looking for a good, experienced teacher, especially one whose name carried a little weight in the publishing world.

Western had asked Lauren to run a creative writing workshop several years ago, when she had won the Behn Foundation Award, but she had been eager to start her second book then and had turned down the offer. A year later, Western had renewed it. She had been on the verge of accepting when Charles had announced that he wanted a divorce. Lauren's friends had encouraged her not to abandon her plans, but she simply forgot to respond until it was too late. Now, she sincerely hoped Western wouldn't hold it against her. A few hours teaching the craft of writing might be the ideal way to hold on to her house.

The next day, sobered by her friends' parting remarks, encouraged by her daughter and armed with budding newfound courage, Lauren called Diane Cart, the head of the writing department, who promptly invited Lauren to a trendy coffee shop near the campus to talk.

Lauren took her time getting ready. She considered this meeting an interview. She carefully sorted through her clothes, seeing, for the first time, some advantage to the extra closet and rack space Charles had left behind. She tried on three trouser suits before finding one that didn't hang on her hips like a sack. But it still needed a belt and was much less flattering than it had once been. She had lost far too much weight recently, but, with the state of her life, she hadn't given a thought to her wardrobe.

Not that Lauren had ever been a woman who turned heads. Although she was tall and toned from exercise, she lacked the hourglass proportions of the ideal female figure. Her breasts were far too small, her behind too big and her waist almost nonexistent. Nonetheless, she had always liked to wear good quality clothes, and she had enjoyed scouring expensive boutiques and department stores in search of them. She hadn't done that since the divorce, but maybe things would change with the interview.

Examining herself in the full-length mirror, Lauren tried not to dwell on the ravages of the past few months. At least, she looked like a professional woman ready for an interview. That was what mattered.

Her gray roots were showing, but that couldn't be helped now. She styled her hair as well as she could and promised herself an appointment at the hairdresser, if she got the job. Then she went to work on her face, hoping to put more sparkle in her blue eyes and more color in her cheeks. She may not have used her makeup kit for a while, but she still knew a few tricks. The woman she saw when she gave herself a final, parting glance in the mirror was not who she used to be, but she wasn't this year's lifeless shadow either.

Diane wasn't at the café when Lauren arrived. She glanced around the room, taking in all the poised, youthful diners, in their twenties and thirties, wearing expensive designer clothes, drinking coffee, reading newspapers or engrossed in flirtatious conversations.

It was like walking onto the set of a fashion shoot. Despite her efforts with her appearance, Lauren felt self-conscious and out of place.

She felt even more drab and dull when Diane Cart swept into the room, looking as if she had stepped off the pages of *Vogue*. Lauren watched Diane cross the room— a self-aware, well-kept, confident woman—and wished she had never made this appointment. She should have waited until she looked less of a wreck. How was she ever going to assert herself to someone like this?

"I'm so sorry I'm late, darling. You can't imagine how busy I am, with the new term beginning and all the meetings I have to attend." Diane leaned over to air-kiss Lauren, enveloping her in perfume. She placed an expensive leather bag on the table, the brand name visible. "The dean has asked me to head another committee. It really is a nuisance. But there you are. I have to do what I have to do. It's so difficult to delegate. I'm sure you understand."

Without bothering to really look at Lauren, Diane waved the waitress over and ordered an espresso.

"One shot. And please make sure it really is only one shot." Turning to Lauren, she said, "Sometimes they add too much water, you know. It tastes like drip coffee. Not at all what I want."

Lauren gave the waitress an apologetic smile, ordered bottled water for herself, then returned her
attention to Diane, who was talking again about the
accumulated responsibilities of her life.

"...and that's why I wanted to see you. I was sure you
would want to contribute to the fund-raiser. I thought
you could do a reading. Maybe present some of your
more recent material. That would be wonderful. I'm
sure everyone would love it."

Lauren had been practically hypnotized by the
brightness of Diane's scarlet nails, so she wasn't sure she
had heard right.

"I'm sorry. Did you invite me here today to discuss a
fund-raiser? For Western University?"

Diane's hand froze in midair. With a smile as stylized
as her dress, she looked at Lauren. "Yes. I was sure you
would want to help."

Lauren laughed without humor. "I think there's
been some misunderstanding. Actually, Diane, I called
because I'm looking for a job. I was wondering if that
workshop you offered me a while ago—two years ago—
was, well, a possibility."

Diane frowned. "You're looking for a job?"

Lauren nodded.

"I'm sorry, Lauren, I'm so sorry. I didn't realize... I
had heard that...but I didn't realize..." Diane waved
her red-tipped fingers in the air to fill in the spaces she
left blank.

Lauren doubted that the woman's sympathetic look was genuine.

"Yes, Diane, I'm looking for a job. With the divorce and everything, I'm a bit short on cash."

"I understand." Diane wrapped a cold hand around Lauren's wrist. Lauren resisted the urge to push it away. She waited to see how understanding the other woman really was.

After a moment, Diane withdrew her hand, leaned back in her chair and sighed heavily. "I realize that it must be really terrible, what you're going through. My husband is such a wonderful man, I can't imagine what it would be like to lose him. But surely you must know that our workshops are planned at least a year in advance. Anyway, after the last offer, I thought you weren't interested."

"I was interested. It was just, well… It was just a bad time for me." Lauren smiled as sweetly as she could. If she concentrated hard enough, she could hold back her tears. She didn't want to cry. She didn't want Diane to know how much she cared. "I guess now is a bad time for you."

"Unfortunately, yes."

"And I don't suppose there would be a teaching position open for the next semester?"

"There might be something, but surely you understand I can't offer you anything, Lauren. It's been several years since you've published, and our students want to be instructed by cutting-edge writers, those who can help them get into print. I don't know if you have that kind of clout anymore."

It took all Lauren's concentration to keep her eyes fixed on Diane's face. Everything inside her was screaming at her to walk away before hearing another humiliating word. But she couldn't leave, not just yet, not without exploring one more possibility.

"I was thinking more on the lines of basic writing skills, composition classes, written expression, that sort of thing."

"When was the last time you taught such a class? Ten years ago?"

Lauren hesitated. She could bend the truth a little, but what was the point? She shook her head. "Longer."

"More than ten years! Lauren, you don't really expect us to hire someone without recent experience? Besides you're overqualified. We rely on our graduate students for those courses, sometimes even the advanced undergrads. They do just fine, especially since they're more in touch with the needs of their peers."

"So there really isn't anything?"

"Not at the moment. But if anything should come up, you'll be the first in mind."

Which was obviously Diane-speak for "Don't hold your breath!"

Clare Hanley pressed the intercom button to address her personal assistant.

"Anything I need to deal with in the next hour or so?"

Anne Wright relayed recent messages, reminded Clare of an upcoming meeting and reported that Anton Muller was waiting to see her. "He wants to go over the McGrady case."

"Send him in. We need to deal with it as soon as possible."

Anton stepped into her office a few moments later, an enormous file under his arm. Clare motioned him toward the table in the corner of the room.

When Anton had joined the firm several years ago, Clare had been skeptical about how they would work together. She had hoped the job would go to one of the women candidates she had been committed to promoting, but, in the end, she'd conceded that Anton's qualifications were strong and his decade-long experience as a Chicago police officer was a considerable asset.

It was his law-enforcement experience that had made her so wary. The firm was already sufficiently testosterone-charged. She really didn't need another junior associate—especially one close to her own age—whose previous profession probably didn't dispose him to taking orders from a woman. For despite all the recent publicity, Chicago's finest could hardly be more gender sensitive than Clare's Ivy League male colleagues. And she knew what Neanderthals they were when it came to working with women, let alone taking directions from one!

So it had come as a complete surprise to discover that Anton was not only an efficient, diligent and cooperative team player, but also extremely respectful of her position and authority. Not that he was a pushover. After working with her on only a couple of cases, he had begun to question her interpretation of the law. Surprised, she had listened to him, and their discussion had shed light on the situation and ultimately helped them to win the case. She appreciated his conviction. She also liked his courteous, diplomatic manner. More and more, she found herself seeking his opinion and collaboration.

This had everything to do with his competence and nothing to do with his looks, she now reminded herself, nothing to do with his broad shoulders and flat stomach and trim waist. Moving toward the table, he turned his back to her, offering her a tantalizing view of a very firm behind, covered in a conservative suit that did nothing to conceal his strong masculinity.

More than once, she had found herself mesmerized by his sleek, pantherlike movements. When she wasn't admiring his gracefulness, she was wondering how his thick hair would feel under her fingers. It was almost as dark as hers, but he had no need to dye the graying streaks. Why should he? They made him look distinguished, nothing like the washed-out, worn-out woman she would be if she didn't make her monthly trips to the hairdresser.

Like her, Anton was single—no family, no significant other of either sex. He always attended office functions solo, as she did. He had joked about it once, suggesting they join forces as the few remaining singles on board. They had laughed loudly and long, but they both knew that was never going to happen. Which was too bad. Because if she didn't have a rule about dating colleagues, he would be first on her list.

"Congratulations, Clare!" He waited for her to sit down before lowering himself into a chair. "I heard about the Dubovski settlement."

She kept her eyes on the table, away from the long, lean legs stretched out in front of her. "Thank you, Anton. I'm pleased with the outcome. It went well for us."

"That's an understatement!" He laughed, and his rugged features softened, making him look younger than the forty-something he was. "Astounding is what everybody else is saying."

She tried to focus on his words, not the vibrant tones of his deep voice. Funny how his voice always sounded so authoritative in court and with clients, when all she could hear in it now were the rich, throaty timbres more fitting for the bedroom.

Clare ignored the tingling sensations spreading from her stomach to her toes. "Congratulations to you, too, Anton," she said, resisting the pull of his blue eyes. "You were a big part of that success."

She worked hard to transmute her face into a patronizing grin, the kind of smile that she used to get from the most senior lawyer in the office when she first joined the firm. Not that Mr. Bailey Senior had had many grins for her. They were reserved for the "boys" who went golfing or fishing with him.

Now Clare allowed herself one last, quick glance at Anton's broad shoulders. Then, bracing herself for the work before them, she reached for the file, her manner all business. "About McGrady vs. McGrady. Have you finished the Preliminary Declaration of Disclosure?"

CHAPTER 3

It took Lauren a day to recover from her disappointing meeting with Diane, thanks to a phone call from Chrissie that prevented her from overindulging in self-pity.

"You can't stop after one failure, Mom," Chrissie had told her. "Do you know how many applications I had to fill out before I got this job? Believe me, I lost count."

"But you're young, Chrissie. You have all the time in the world. You could afford to wait for your dream position. I can't. I've got bills closing in on me."

"It's not all happening tomorrow," Chrissie said with the same conviction she'd used to get her position as legal advisor for an international organization. "You can still call around."

"But Diane said—"

"Forget Diane, Mom. So she wasn't helpful. So it didn't work out at Western. Do you know how many universities and colleges there are in the Chicago area?"

"I know, sweetheart. But it's not me they want."

"Oh, Mom! All of them would kill to have you!"

Not Western apparently. "Sweetheart—"

"Do you want me to come back and do it for you, Mom? I will if I have to. Don't think I won't."

Lauren was touched by her daughter's concern. Chrissie had done so much for her since the divorce. She had even been ready to give up the job she had been after ever since she'd graduated from law school. But Lauren had put her foot down and insisted she would be fine.

She was going to have to do the same thing now, although it meant agreeing to make those calls. Besides, she didn't have the energy to argue with her daughter. Even with an ocean and a continent separating them, Chrissie was more formidable than a steamroller. No wonder she'd gotten the position she'd wanted.

"Okay, I'll do it," Lauren said, trying to sound enthusiastic.

"Great, Mom."

But after her sixth rejection, Lauren felt she would have been better off not complying. No one she spoke with was as intimidating as Diane, but the responses were all pretty much the same. There were no positions open for the coming semester. Budget constraints were so severe, some of the staff would have to be cut. Either Lauren was overqualified for teaching introductory writing courses or she wasn't experienced enough. For some recruiters, she was too prestigious for their school's humble programs. For others, she lacked the snappy, experimental and contemporary style their students coveted.

Whichever way she looked, she was wrong for the job. So now she wasn't only a has-been writer and a failed wife, she was also a no-go writing teacher!

Lauren wasn't ready to risk any more rejection, especially suspecting that the acceptances were going to kids who could barely sign their names when she had had her first articles published. She almost didn't tell Chrissie. Her daughter was bound to encourage her to keep trying with other schools. But when she asked, Lauren couldn't lie. She wasn't about to break one of the fundamental rules of parenting over this.

Surprisingly, Chrissie didn't press the issue.

"Never mind about teaching, Mom," she said, her voice as clear as if she were standing next to her. "Sell your talents at writing."

What do you think I have been trying to do? Lauren wanted to scream, but she swallowed the retort. Chrissie was trying so hard to be encouraging. The least Lauren could do was play the game.

"And who would want to hire me? Unless you know someone who wants his family history written. Or maybe some love letters," she added, thinking of one of Chrissie's favorite films. "No. Forget that. I'm no Cyrano de Bergerac."

Chrissie laughed. "Not love letters, Mom, but online dating profiles. Now that's an idea. In fact—"

"A bad idea," Lauren intervened before her daughter

could go any further. "I don't even know what they are. Seriously, Chrissie—"

"Seriously, Mom. Maybe you're no Cyrano, but people do hire writers. Businesses need writers. So do nonprofit organizations. We just hired someone to write a ten-page brochure for us. That's what made me think of you. It's the sort of thing you could do easily. You did it for Dad for years without getting paid. In fact, come to think of it, after you put together a writing portfolio, you might contact some of his colleagues and see if they're interested."

"What a good idea, Chrissie!" Lauren said, pressing hard on her lips so she wouldn't yell with exasperation.

Because, of course, it was a terrible idea. Perhaps Charles's colleagues would send some work her way, but it would be as a favor to her ex-husband, the kind of favor she could do without. She wouldn't put what little dignity she had up for sale.

But, she realized after she and Chrissie had said their goodbyes, she wasn't ready to give up her house, either. She might not want to contact Charles's friends, but Chrissie did have a point: there must be someone out there who could use her gift with words. Just because she couldn't land a teaching job didn't mean she couldn't write. Just because she was having problems with her book didn't mean she couldn't work on someone else's.

She was having a run of bad luck, but she could turn

things around. Hadn't she restored the house on her own while taking care of two toddlers? Hadn't she written a prize-winning book while raising rebellious teenagers? She'd managed fine without Charles then. She could do it again. She would find a way to meet her payments. There must be a writing job out there for her. All she had to do was spread her net a bit wider.

Clare made her way down the sidewalk and cursed the infamous Chicago wind. In her light jacket and thin silk stockings, she wasn't prepared for the sudden chill of the early spring night. Luckily, the restaurant was only several steps away. She hurried through the swinging doors and crossed the room slowly, examining the crowd carefully.

No sign of Harry. His description didn't fit any of the men leaning against the bar. Nor was he waiting at any of the booths.

She wasn't surprised. She was late.

She had been running all day. First to a meeting that she had almost missed because the "boys" had conveniently forgotten to mention it to her. No surprise there, either. Even after all these years, they still didn't accept her as one of their own. As long as she didn't golf with them, laugh at their sexist jokes, or share the same illustrious pedigree, they never would.

Fortunately, Bailey Junior, hardly the biggest brain around, had let something slip. Just as well, because if

Clare hadn't been there, the "boys" would have assigned the Van Belden account to one of the incompetent young associates who smooched up to them on the golf course. She had offered to do some of the screening. More work for her, for sure, but how else was she going to get the firm to look at the women candidates?

After the meeting, she'd had to race across town for her weekly session with the law students she mentored. She couldn't let those women down, not knowing first-hand how high the cards were stacked against them. Which was also why Clare had stayed longer than she should have.

Then, it was back to the office again to file a custody petition. It had to be in as soon as possible. It wasn't about advancing her career and billing more hours. It was about children, getting them out of a bad situation and sparing them as much grief as possible. Anyone would understand why she had to stay after hours.

But apparently Harry hadn't. She was twenty minutes late, and it looked like he was long gone. That would teach her to put obligations before pleasure. That would teach her to put her clients first and men after. She should have learned that lesson a long time ago.

Still, nothing was stopping her from having a little pleasure on her own. She would have a drink before she headed home, two if she was up for it. Which was not likely, nor advisable. She had known how unadvisable before most kids could read.

Still, nothing wrong with one drink. Just one drink and then she'd head home. Alone. Again.

Clare found an empty seat at the bar and ordered a martini. While she waited, she checked her cell phone. Harry had called to tell her he wasn't waiting. Too bad for him. She didn't care. She certainly didn't need him. There were others like him out there, and even if there weren't, it didn't matter.

She liked being single, most of the time anyway. She could call the shots. Eat in or eat out—as she wanted. Decide where to vacation and what car to buy. She had no regrets and no heartbreaks. Not recently anyway and certainly nothing like Lauren.

Poor woman! She was going to have to rebuild her whole life at an age when most women just wanted to lie back and enjoy. No wonder Lauren was feeling so down lately. A new job could only help, if not for her house, then at least for herself.

Clare snapped her phone shut and slipped it back into her purse. She toyed with her martini as she slowly eyed the men around the bar. She could give them more attention now that she knew she was on her own.

After a day like today, she didn't have the energy to pick up anyone, but there was nothing wrong with looking. Everything was so much easier when only window-shopping was involved. She didn't have to worry about sagging breasts, cellulite dimples and wrinkled skin. And there would be no chance of being stood up if she put her work first.

So, let's see. Who's going to be the lucky guy tonight? Not the boy with wind-swept blond hair. She didn't want to be accused of cradle-robbing. Not Mr. Marlboro in the corner there, either. He would spend too much time admiring himself in the mirror. Which maybe wasn't such a bad idea because he wouldn't have any time to notice her bulges. Then again, if she was going to do this, she wanted to feel good about herself. So forget Mr. Marlboro.

Clare sipped her martini and continued to scan the candidates. Not Mr. Junior Exec. She'd had enough of his type in the courtroom today. Mr. Sensitive with Glasses and Long Hair wouldn't do, either. He probably wouldn't approve of her constant wrangling over financial settlements. Of course, she wouldn't want to spend too much time discussing them with him. She had other plans in mind. Plans for his long hair and his nice-looking mouth. Too bad he was a sensitive type.

Clare sighed and sipped again. There was no pleasing her tonight. Maybe she should look at the booths. Maybe she—

"Clare?"

She turned in the direction of the familiar voice.

"Oh, hello, Anton."

Like her, he hadn't changed out of his business suit.

But he had taken off his blazer and was carrying it, hooked on a finger, over his shoulder in a careless manner she found sexy. He had removed his tie, and had loosened the top buttons of his shirt, revealing dark chest hairs. She swallowed—discretely she hoped—and forced her eyes up toward his sea-blue eyes and slightly weathered face.

With his good-guy looks and well-toned body, Anton was a far better proposition than anything else she had seen so far. She was hard-pressed to find anything wrong with him.

Oh, yes. There was something, something very wrong. He was a lawyer and he worked for her.

"What are you doing here?" she asked.

"That was going to be my line." He smiled at her, and she wished more than ever that she didn't have a rule about relationships with colleagues. "I thought you were working late tonight. Your door was shut when I left, or I would have asked if you wanted to join me."

"I would have said 'no.' I was supposed to meet someone here, but I think I was stood up."

She twisted her head over her shoulder as if to give the room another look, but she really just wanted to increase the space between them.

"His loss." Anton brought his hand down, draping his blazer over his other arm. He tilted his head toward the stool next to her. "Mind if I join you?"

"You're on your own?"

"Not if I'm here with you," he teased. "I came with some friends, but they're leaving."

He waved to a group of several men and women who were exiting. Clare was relieved to see there was no one from Bailey, Brooks, Kantowicz and Hanley. Office gossips would have a field day with this encounter, not to mention the martini she had practically guzzled.

He looked down at her, waiting for an answer.

"You know," she said, blinking to avoid the blue of his eyes. "We never celebrated the Dubovski victory. Let me buy you this drink."

He hesitated, then nodded. "Sure. If you'll let me get the next round."

"It's a deal."

She waved at Jimmy the bartender, wondering at the wisdom of what she was doing. She hadn't eaten anything since a sandwich at lunchtime and she was beginning to feel light-headed. But she and Anton did have something to celebrate, and Clare had never properly expressed her appreciation. What was a drink between colleagues?

She ordered her second martini. It was exactly what she wanted, strong and pungent, the kind of cocktail her father always drank. His preferences had certainly given her a lifelong taste for the stuff, as well as a deep-rooted revulsion.

Jimmy put their drinks down. She reached for her glass.

"To Mrs. Dubovski. Let's hope she's much happier without Mr."

Without waiting for Anton's response, Clare drank her martini like she might lemonade on a humid Chicago summer afternoon. Anton had a sip of whatever he was drinking, his eyes never leaving her.

"Are you okay?" He put a hand on her shoulder.

She could feel the heat of his hand through the silk of her blouse. Was it the alcohol that was burning her, or something else?

"Fine." She shrugged off his hand. "Just fine. Nothing another shot of gin won't help. If I'd known this bar had become so stingy with the drinks, I wouldn't have stayed. Come on, drink up, Anton. We have another round to go."

But Anton took his sweet time, rolling his glass between his hands, tilting it against his lips, rubbing it against his mouth. Clare tried not to look, but it was hard. And her alcohol haze didn't help.

On the contrary. It was a great boost to lowering her inhibitions, to helping her imagine something else in the place of that glass—like her lips or her face or her breasts.

Those thoughts were enough to send heat like flames up her whole body. She shut her eyes to chase the images away, but they only appeared ten times more vivid.

Anton finally put his empty glass down.

"Good! You're done!" Clare said. "Now, let's see if

we can get Jimmy to look this way. You'd think he'd know me by now, after all the times I've been here and all the tips I've left."

"I think he's having the same thoughts I am." Anton stared at the empty glass that she was clutching.

"And what would those be?" She looked up at him. His face was blurry and unclear.

"That you've had too much to drink as it is," he said in the same matter-of-fact tone he used when advising a client.

Without another word, he took her glass away from her and emptied the little that was left into his own. She didn't have the energy to protest. She just looked at him as he pushed off the bar and straightened to his full six foot three. She had to tilt her head all the way back to see his face. It took her several seconds to make out his concerned expression.

"He's not worth it, Clare. Whoever he is. If he stood you up like this, he must be a jerk."

If she weren't so dizzy, she might have burst out laughing. Sweet of Anton, but much too earnest and wholesome for a lawyer and an ex-cop. Yet she really could get a rush from the way he was looking at her. Maybe she could talk him into adoring her body—minus the sags, the cellulite and the wrinkles—but she'd have to open her mouth and move her tongue. She closed her eyes and concentrated very hard.

"Save it," she managed. "I know all about jerks."

"And not enough about good guys. They do exist, you know."

"Not in my world."

"Maybe it's time you tried mine."

Clare wasn't sure she had heard right or that she understood what he was saying. She turned her head so quickly, the room spun around her. She reached for the bar to steady herself. Somehow, she found herself leaning against Anton, enveloped in the scent of his aftershave, his warmth and his strength. She didn't move for a moment. Comforted by his steadying hand, she turned her head to look up at him again. His mouth was close. All she had to do was lift her lips a bit, and they would be kissing.

Kissing? No kissing. No kissing Anton.

She drew her head back instead, her hand grasping the bar tightly. She needed to leave before she did something stupid, but she didn't know if she *could* leave. Hell, she didn't even know if she could stand straight. Her head sagged forward. The world spun around her in a kaleidoscope of faces, forms and objects. Her ears registered sounds without meaning. She felt Anton's hand on her shoulder.

"Are you sure you're all right, Clare? Can I do anything?"

She stared at him for an instant, and then suddenly the sound of clinking glasses, conversation and laughter from a nearby booth broke through her haze. With it came an embarrassed awareness of where she was and what was wrong with her.

She pulled away from him. Wouldn't the office gossips have a field day with this?

"Clare, I—"

She wanted to shake her head, but she was too dizzy. "I think you'd better call me a cab," she said, her voice as clear and firm as on her best day in court.

Lauren considered the letter she had just drafted. It sounded professional, efficient and convincing. Surely one of the names she had gotten off the online job listing that Chrissie had given her would belong to someone who would want to hire her as a writer. But what did she know? It had been such a long time since she had written such a letter, she really had no idea what was right. Business etiquette couldn't have changed that much, but after her dreadful encounter with Diane and all the other demoralizing rejections she'd received, Lauren didn't know. She needed another opinion.

Lauren glanced at her watch. Too late to contact Chrissie. It was already ten in the evening in Vienna. Clare was a better bet. She was always hiring people. And didn't she mentor a group of female law students? Clare must give out this kind of advice all the time. She could do the same for Lauren.

Lauren dialed the number, but the machine picked

up. Clare was probably at her office. It wouldn't be the first time she worked on the weekend. Lauren wouldn't disturb her there, but she decided to try Alice.

Alice may not be as much in the know as Clare, but she wasn't totally ignorant either. However Lauren was in for another rude surprise when instead of her friend's usual warm greeting, Alice practically barked hello into the phone.

"It's me, Alice. Lauren. Are you, um, all right?"

"Yes, yes, I'm fine," Alice answered through what sounded like gritted teeth. "What do you want?"

"If it's a bad time, I can call back."

"That's okay. I'm fine."

There was a long pause, in which Lauren heard muffled sounds, as if Alice were exhaling loudly. When her friend spoke again, she sounded more like her usual self.

"I'm sorry, Lauren. It's… I… You just caught me at a bad moment."

"No, I'm sorry. I don't mean to bother you. I can always—"

"I said it's okay. What gives?"

Suspecting that this really wasn't a good time, Lauren tried to put off the conversation, but Alice wouldn't have it. So, after apologizing for being such a nuisance, she explained what she wanted. Alice suggested they meet at a coffee shop in Oak Park later that afternoon.

"Are you sure Frank won't mind?" Lauren asked.

"I know you like to spend your weekends together. Family time, you call it."

"Frank? I doubt he'd even notice," Alice replied in unusually strident tones.

Of course, Frank would notice. He and Alice were inseparable. But, later thinking over this strange conversation, Lauren recalled Alice's cryptic remarks at lunch the other day. She wondered what was going on. Had she been so self-absorbed she hadn't seen what was happening to her oldest and dearest friend? She resolved to find out.

So in the coffee shop, after they had gone over her résumé and her cover letter, Lauren asked, "How are things with you? Everything okay?"

"Everything's fine," Alice responded, a bit too quickly and curtly for Lauren's liking.

"Sure? No problems at work?"

Alice shook her head.

"With the children?"

"The kids are fine. Everything's fine."

"Frank?"

"He's fine. Honestly, Lauren, everything is fine."

"I'm just asking. You sounded funny earlier, and I was surprised you agreed to come today. Not that I don't appreciate it. But this was always your time for Frank, the kids and you."

Lauren had always envied the way Alice and Frank had done things together. Despite their different careers, upbringings and philosophies, they had placed the children at the center of their lives, making their family a shared priority. Frank took them to sports practice, and Alice took them to music lessons. They took turns overseeing their homework.

That had definitely not been the case with Charles and Lauren. The kids and the house had been her responsibility. Even on weekends, Charles had been too busy to make time for his wife and children. Or, as Lauren had come to learn, too bored and uninterested to bother with anything they might enjoy. In the end, she had stopped asking and had organized things just for the children and herself.

"Things change," Alice said. "It happens, as you know."

"Change? How?" Lauren felt a cold hand squeezing her heart. Frank and Alice had always had such a great relationship. It couldn't be falling apart now.

"Well, the children are gone, for one," Alice replied. "So I guess we're experiencing some growing pains."

"Growing pains? But you're all grown-up."

Alice sighed. "Doesn't mean we've stopped sprouting. We still need our weeding and pruning."

"At least, you're growing in the same direction."

When Alice didn't say anything, Lauren couldn't stop herself from asking, "You are, aren't you?"

Alice stirred her coffee slowly, seemingly enthralled by the tiny ripples forming on the surface. "I hope so. But sometimes I wonder. We don't do anything together anymore. We could be living on opposite sides of the continent, of the globe, for that matter. It wouldn't be any different." She set the spoon down on the saucer and folded her arms across her chest. "You know why we're not together today? Because he can't tear himself away from the TV! Can you imagine? The kids had to fight to get a TV because he thought they were already far too brainwashed without one, and now he can't turn it off? I don't get it. I just don't."

Lauren remembered those arguments. Frank's disapproval of the mainstream media and entertainment industry was one of the last remaining testimonies to his radical past. For years, until they were teenagers, Karen and Mark would come to Lauren's house to watch their favorite shows. "Like you said, things change."

Alice's only response was a grunt.

"I guess that means you're not too interested in watching TV."

Alice's raised eyebrow was answer enough.

"I guess not. Well then, maybe you need to find something that will get Frank away from it. Think of something you can do together. In the meantime, let's do something for ourselves, and I know just the thing. In fact, I'm going to make a salon appointment for both of us."

Several days after that appointment, Lauren still wasn't used to the face in the mirror. She'd only wanted to get her roots retouched, but the stylist had convinced her to cut it short. Very short. Lauren's hair hadn't been shorter than a chin-length bob since college, and even that had been difficult for her in the beginning.

But the stylist had said something about a short, spunky look taking some of the droop off her face, and Alice would only agree to try new highlights in her hair if she had a partner in crime. With such persuasive opposition, what could Lauren do but give in?

Now, she rubbed gel into her hands and worked it into her hair the way she'd been shown. Who would think that she would be trying this goop for the first time at fifty-three? Wouldn't Chrissie be surprised? Probably. But she would approve.

The droop was still there, Lauren thought, noticing the circles under her eyes. But the close-cropped style did give her a dignity and grace that she had thought lost forever. Now, all she needed was a life to go with the look.

If only everything were as simple as a haircut, but both she and Alice knew it wasn't. They had brainstormed a list of activities that might seduce Frank away from his newfound love, the television, and back into the arms of his decades-old wife. Lauren hoped one of their ideas would work. And if it didn't, she'd be there for her friend.

She was still considering her new face when the doorbell rang. She wasn't expecting anyone. It was a bit too soon for a response to those applications she had sent out, but maybe she was finally getting lucky.

She ran downstairs and opened the door.

* * *

"Hello, Helen," Lauren said to Chrissie's former roommate, taking in the short form standing on her porch. A dark ski cap was pulled low over the young woman's face, covering her hair. It made her eyes very blue and her elfin features pronounced. Unfortunately, with her oversized down-jacket, she looked more like a troll than an elf.

"Hello, Lauren. Do you—" Helen stopped and stared. "You've done something to your hair. It looks very different," she said. "Very nice, I mean. I like it."

"Thank you, Helen." Without thinking, Lauren reached up and touched the spiky tufts of hair.

What could Helen Matter want? Surely she knew Chrissie was in Vienna. Maybe she was looking for Jeff. Helen's crush on Lauren's son had always been so transparent. Lauren had wanted to teach a poor girl a thing or two about men, but given how badly Lauren had misjudged the man in her life, Helen would probably be better off learning those lessons herself.

"Do you, um, mind if I come in?"

Realizing they had been standing silent for the last minute, Lauren nodded and pulled the door open. It was then she realized that Helen had come with two big suitcases, a duffel bag and a leather carry-on the size of a laptop. If the baggage was anything to judge by, Helen wasn't just coming in. She was moving in.

Trying to make sense of it all, Lauren forgot to ask Helen if she wanted any help. Before she knew it, everything was inside, neatly stacked at the bottom of the oak staircase.

"Helen?"

The young woman turned around, an anxious look on her face. "Don't worry. I'll carry it all up. I really won't get in your way."

"In my way?"

"Yes. It'll all go to Chrissie's room."

"Chrissie's room?"

"Yes. Chrissie's room," Helen said, pulling off her ski cap. Her long blond hair clung to her face. She brushed it away as a hint of a smile started to show. It faded quickly in response to Lauren's puzzled expression.

"Oh my God! She didn't tell you? She said she would. I wouldn't have come otherwise. Oh my God! She said it would be all right. She said you wouldn't mind. Oh my God! She said—"

"Wouldn't mind about what? I'm afraid you've lost me completely here. What's going on?" Lauren shook her head in confusion.

"Chrissie said you agreed. I wouldn't have come otherwise. She said she talked to you—"

"Talked to me about *what*?"

"She said it was okay—"

"Helen—"

Something in Lauren's voice must have finally broken through. Helen stopped rambling. She took a deep breath. "I guess she didn't tell you."

"No. But you could. I would like that."

"I don't have any place to stay. My roommate and my boyfriend—well, he's not my boyfriend, really. My roommate and a guy, a guy I know, well they, um, they…" Her arms flailed around helplessly. "Well, anyway, he may be moving in. And, um, there isn't enough room for the three of us, so I had to leave. I've tried campus housing and the Internet, but there's nothing. Not until September. Chrissie said I could stay here until then. She said you wouldn't mind, Lauren. I wouldn't have come otherwise. Really, I wouldn't—"

Lauren held up her hand, signaling Helen to stop. She'd had enough of the hysterical ranting for one day, especially since she still didn't understand what was going on.

"Didn't they give you any notice?"

"Notice? Oh you mean about the apartment? No, the lease is in my name."

"Then why are you leaving?"

Lauren didn't know why she was asking. Helen may have been a child prodigy. She might be brushing shoulders with Nobel Prize winners. She might even be a future prize-winner herself. But she had very little idea how to deal with the real world.

"It's easier for one person to leave than for two."

"And they wanted you to leave straight away?"

"No, but it was kind of awkward. They—"

Lauren held up her hand again. She didn't want to

hear any more details. "So Chrissie told you that you could use her room?"

"Yes. Until I find something else. I'll pay you, of course. Chrissie said you, um, needed the money. With the divorce and everything."

So that's why Chrissie hadn't bothered to tell her! She was interfering in her mother's life! She thought she had found the perfect solution for everyone. Never mind that Lauren wasn't interested in sharing her house again!

She liked living alone. Well, not really. The house was so big, empty and gloomy now. Still, she was getting used to it, and she really didn't want to share her life and her habits with a roommate. She didn't need an outsider observing her emotions, invading her space and interrupting her routine. She hadn't liked group living arrangements when she was younger and she wasn't about to try again. Home was for family, not for strangers who walked in off the street.

But, Lauren suddenly remembered, she didn't have a family, not one that lived here anyway. And Helen wasn't a stranger. Lauren had known her for almost ten years, ever since the girls were freshmen in college. Lauren had warmed to Helen then, despite her rather odd behavior. Chrissie knew this. She also knew her mother would never chase her best friend away, no matter how much she wanted to.

"Okay, Helen," Lauren said. "You can stay."

"I can stay?"

"Yes. In Chrissie's room," Lauren said, resigned to the fact that even with continents and oceans separating them, her daughter was formidable.

CHAPTER 4

What was Clare going to do?

In fifteen minutes, Anton Muller was going to walk through that door with a file under his arm and questions in his eye. Questions? She would be lucky if there were just questions. More like accusations, recriminations, condemnations.

No matter. He could hardly have more than she did. For several days now, she had been reminding herself of everything she had done wrong. And when she was done, she had begun all over again. She had acted like an out-of-control twenty-year-old.

Clare closed her eyes tightly, hoping the waves of embarrassment and regret would wash away. They didn't. This problem was much harder to fix than her Saturday-morning hangover.

Breathe deep. Inhale. Exhale. Inhale. Exhale. Good. Now think, calmly, rationally, the way you do when preparing a brief. The way you do in court. Just think.

Think? How was she going to sit next to Anton, calmly discussing depositions, custody feuds and marital settlement agreements? Could she look him in the face and not remember that he had seen her drunk? Could she sit next to him and forget what it had been like to be held in his arms? Could she hand him the file and ignore that her whole body had ached for him? Was still aching for him.

Fool. Idiot. Behaving like a lovesick teenager.

No wonder there were rules! Thou shalt not get drunk with thy colleague. Thou shalt not covet thy colleague. Even when his face is a fraction of an inch away from yours and his aftershave fills your nose. Even when his arms are wrapped around you. Even when he covets you, too.

No. Forget that. Anton didn't covet her. She was all the more the fool if she thought that the case. And even if he did, she was at fault here. She and she alone. Anton had just been kind and helpful and supportive, as always. The way he had been when he had put her in a cab and sent her home.

Drunk. Humiliated. Mortified.

Why had she ignored the rules? Why now? Why with Anton?

What if the office gossips got hold of this! Clare could already hear the whispers. She could see the smirking looks. She could feel the accusatory labels. She couldn't let it happen. Ever.

There was an easy way to do it. What Bailey Senior had done with Jenny What's-Her-Name. Pull Anton off all the cases they worked together. Ignore him. Stonewall him into leaving the firm if necessary. Make him pay for her hormones and her absent self-control. She could do that.

No. No. No. She couldn't do that. She was responsible for what happened—for what almost happened. She would have to deal with it. She would have to talk to him. Then, they could bury it together. Forever.

Lauren lifted the spoon from the counter and plunged it into the sugar bowl. She then transferred the bowl to the far end of the shelf, placing it next to the other condiments. She fiddled with the other containers, alphabetizing and aligning them into neat and orderly rows.

Some might call her obsessive, but after thirty years of running her own house she knew exactly what it should look like because she knew exactly where everything should be. Her husband and her children had respected that. Why couldn't Helen do the same?

Ever since the young woman had moved in a week ago, Lauren had done nothing but tidy up and set things straight. Helen didn't have any eye for the order that Lauren had established in her house, the order she liked to keep. How had Chrissie managed to live with Helen? But then Chrissie hadn't always been too keen about her mother's rigid housekeeping. No wonder the two girls had roomed together for so long.

With a sigh, Lauren picked up the dishcloth Helen had left on the table and placed it on the rack. She didn't think she would be able to continue with this living arrangement much longer. She wasn't ready to do a remake of *The Odd Couple*.

It didn't matter that Helen had said she would stick to Chrissie's room. She had to cook and to eat and to bathe. To do that, she had to venture into other parts of the house. The parts Lauren thought of as "hers," but which were rapidly becoming Helen's.

Of course, Helen didn't realize what she was doing when she forgot to return the spoon to the sugar bowl or left the kitchen tap running, or stomped mud on the porch instead of on the mat.

They were little things, irrelevant things. But they irritated Lauren all the more because she couldn't complain about them. Who could she complain to, anyway? Helen would certainly apologize and then she would forget what she had done. Chrissie would snort and tell her mother to get on with it, just as she had done when Lauren had confronted her about Helen's surprise arrival.

"It's for your own good," she had said.

"You seem to be forgetting who you are talking to, Chrissie. I'm the mother in this relationship. *I* watch out for *your* good. Not the other way round."

"We already tried that. Now it's my turn. Oh, and Mom, what's this about a haircut?"

"Alice and I decided to try something new," Lauren began only to realize what her daughter was up to. "But Chrissie—"

"Helen says it looks nice."

"Chrissie—"

"Oh, come on, Mom. She needs a place to stay, you need some money."

"I don't need strangers in the house."

"She's not a stranger. She's almost family."

"Not family, Chrissie. She's a friend."

"A very dear friend. Practically a sister. Surely you can adopt her for a while? After Jeff and me, it shouldn't be that big a deal."

Actually, it was a big deal. It was hard enough for Lauren to take care of herself. How could she take on Helen as well? But Lauren let it go. At least it was for a good cause. The rent money would buy her a little more time with the house.

Anton knocked on the door and entered without waiting. Clare joined him at the table and pulled the file he had placed there toward her. She tapped her fingers against it, but didn't open it. Instead she forced herself to look straight into his mesmerizing deep blue eyes.

"Anton," she said, stretching as tall as she could, trying to be as imposing as her five feet seven inch height would allow. "About what happened the other night… I just… I just wanted to say thank-you. For getting me a cab, I mean."

"I'm glad I could be there for you. You must have had some hangover."

He ruffled his peppered hair and gave her an endearing, boyish grin. She almost forgot all her best-laid plans.

"It was pretty bad. But I've learned my lesson. I'm sorry you had to deal with it."

Anton leaned forward, his hands reaching for hers, but she pulled away. He slumped back in his chair.

"There's nothing to be sorry for. I'm glad I could be there for you."

"There is every reason."

"Clare—"

"I have certain responsibilities here. To the firm. To you as my associate. I was, I was, well, not quite myself." She smiled nervously, then breathed deeply. "It won't happen again."

He seemed about to say something, but changed his mind. "Sure. I understand."

"Thank you." She exhaled. Then, she thought of something else. "Oh, and Anton, I would appreciate it if…"

"Don't worry. I have no intention of telling anybody. Believe me, I would never do that, Clare."

"Thank you," she said, ignoring the way he made her name sounded like a caress. "I appreciate it. It would be best for both of us if we pretend it never happened."

Gazing at the bookcase behind her, Anton nodded, almost as if he hadn't registered what she was saying, as if it didn't matter.

She was more than happy to leave it at that. She put

her hands against the table, pulled her chair in and opened the file. "Now about that deposition…"

Lauren sat at the breakfast table and picked up the newspaper pages scattered across the top. Couldn't Helen have put them in the recycling bin, instead of cluttering the place with them?

Well, since the paper was still here, Lauren might as well take a look. She browsed through the sections rapidly, pausing when she came to the entertainment news. She wondered if she should call Alice and tell her about the review of the documentary film. It was the sort of thing Frank liked, and it just might get him out of the house. So far Alice's attempts hadn't been too successful, but she had to keep on trying.

Lauren picked up the phone to call her friend when something in the classifieds caught her eye. She sat down to read.

"Oh, hi, Lauren," Helen said from the doorway. "You haven't seen a yellow-covered book have you? I can't find it anywhere."

Probably because you left it lying somewhere, anywhere, Lauren wanted to retort. But because she didn't want to reveal her annoyance, she lifted the pages off the table to show Helen that nothing was hidden from view. "It's not here."

"Oh, well. It'll show up."

It sure will. Under your bed. Or in my bookcase. Or

behind one of the cushions on the living room couch. Anywhere but where it's supposed to be.

"There are some good ideas there, aren't there?" Helen was saying, pointing to the pages in Lauren's hand. "I mean, I've been wearing my old jeans for so long I never knew I could try something else."

She giggled self-consciously. Lauren stared at her, noticing for the first time the change in Helen's usual androgynous uniform. Instead of an oversized shirt and faded jeans, she wore a pink woolen skirt and a cream-colored blouse, the kind Lauren's mother or grandmother might have worn. Helen's blond hair was pulled back in a tight bun, which gave her a very severe appearance. She looked different. But she didn't look good.

"I'm trying to change my image," Helen explained, noting Lauren's speculative glance. "I'm trying something different. Something more, you know, with it. But I'm not sure this is me, either."

She seemed so insecure that Lauren didn't think she could break the truth to her. She never would have thought someone as smart as Helen would have such a hard time figuring out what looked good on her. Should she say something, push Helen in the right direction for this makeover she was longing for? Maybe she could send her to the stylist who had worked wonders for her and Alice. Lauren decided against it. She had tried with Chrissie, and it hadn't been appreciated.

"How are you otherwise?" she asked to change the

subject. She instantly regretted it because Helen was just waiting for the invitation to sit down and talk. To tell Lauren why she wanted to change her image and what a shame it was that Chrissie wasn't here to help her do it. How she had signed up for a series of seminars on how to improve her dating strategy because she had such a hard time giving off the right signals and an even harder time understanding the signals men gave her. She was also planning to write a profile of herself to post on an online dating service and could Lauren please take a look at it.

Lauren nodded, wondering whether to volunteer help.

"Of course," she said in a polite, neutral voice. "Just show it to me when you're ready, and I'll see what I can do. There's something here I'd like to look into. Do you mind if I keep it?" She tapped the pages in front of her.

"Sure."

Helen left to continue her search for her misplaced book. Lauren removed one page from the employment section and placed the rest in the corner with the other papers to be recycled. Perhaps this was the job she had been waiting for. Perhaps her good deed would be rewarded after all.

"So, Mom, did you apply for the job at the *Chicago Gazette?*" Chrissie asked, as soon as they had exchanged their usual greetings.

"I…" Lauren began, but couldn't continue.

"Did you, Mom?"

With her free hand, Lauren fingered the framed photograph in front of her. Chrissie's smiling face, capped with Lauren's chestnut hair and reflecting Charles's dark eyes, stared back at her. Lauren was in the habit of addressing the photo whenever she spoke to her daughter on the phone.

The picture had been taken shortly after Chrissie's college graduation. It captured the young woman in all the eagerness of youth, still fresh from her entry into the adult world, so ready to confront the challenges the universe offered. The girl in the photo simply could not imagine the smallest obstacle in the new, exciting path to glory that she was just beginning. Lauren couldn't remember the last time she had felt that way.

"Chrissie, I don't think it's the right job for me. It's a singles column."

"So? You're single."

"I'm not. I mean I *am* single, but I'm not *that* kind of single."

"And how many different kinds are there? You're either single or you're not."

"Actually, if the census bureau is anything to go by, there's more than one kind. You can be single or you can be separated, divorced or widowed."

"So you're the divorced kind of single. What's the problem?"

"The problem is I'm not the Carrie-Bradshaw-and-her-friends kind of single. That's what they're looking for. Someone to write witty, self-deprecating commentary on the single woman's relentless pursuit of happiness."

"Sounds like you, Mom."

"Right. If you believe that, you don't know your mother anymore."

"I know my mother. She's the one who's forgotten who she is."

Lauren didn't know how such an intelligent person managed to hold on to all her illusions.

"Seriously, Chrissie. I'm not a young, optimistic thirty-something. I'm an aging, wrinkled, bitter and de-pressed fifty-something who no longer believes happiness is to be found in expensive shoes, endless cocktails, low-cal salad dressing and a man who is waiting for me some-where, out there, at the other side of a crowded club."

"Well, part of what you're saying is true. You're cer-tainly not thirty, and you probably have a different recipe for happiness. But I, for one, would be interested in finding out where you and your friends would look for love. It wouldn't be *Sex and the City*, but that's old, anyway."

"Not as old as I am."

"Sorry, Mom, but nothing is as old as old news and old television shows. I'm surprised the *Gazette* doesn't know that. I mean, we already know about the life and times of thirty-somethings, thanks to Bridget Jones, Carrie Bradshaw, Ally McBeal and Grace. What about the forty- and fifty-somethings?"

Lauren sighed. "If my life is anything to go by, it would make an extremely boring column. And a very depressing one. Who wants to hear another story about a has-been writer dumped for a younger woman?"

"Didn't that happen to Carrie? With a twenty-year-old? She pulled through, though, didn't she?"

"Her breasts aren't sagging, she looks great in a knee-length skirt and she doesn't have a daughter almost as old as the other woman who gives her bad professional advice."

"Oh, Mom, that's not what it's all about," Chrissie said. "There are a lot of women—and men—out there whose bodies are in worse shape than yours. They don't give up. I've already told you that one of my professors is just dying to meet you. You're the one who isn't interested. And, anyway, it's not just about finding a man. There's a whole lot more to being single. At twenty, at thirty, at forty and definitely at fifty. It would make a great column. It wouldn't be Carrie and the girls, but it would be fun. You should do it, Mom. You really should."

Lauren's right hand was beginning to feel numb. Another sign of age. She shifted the phone to the other hand before she spoke again.

"Chrissie, this is the *Chicago Gazette* we're talking about, not *Good Housekeeping* or *O*. Don't you understand? It would be like having Dear Abby write about Harley-Davidsons. I'm not the person they want. Really. I'm not."

"Did they say that?"

"No. They don't have to. Haven't you been listening to me?"

"Of course, Mom. I always listen to you."

Lauren could hear the teasing tone. She looked at the brown eyes smiling back at her in the photograph and imagined them widening as Chrissie acted out the part of the obedient daughter. But the person on the other end of the line was not obedient; she was persistent.

"So you haven't even called them for information?"

"Actually, I have. They asked me to send a sample of my writing and my ideas for the column."

"Not your résumé? If they saw that, it would clinch it."

"That's the other thing, Chrissie. They're looking for someone relatively unknown. But Lauren Gard is already known."

For the first time that evening, there was a long moment of silence at the other end. But although Chrissie stalled, she wasn't giving up.

"Lauren Gard is. But Lauren Wilt isn't."

It took Lauren a moment to understand what Chrissie was suggesting. She wasn't sure it would be completely honest or entirely legal to use the maiden name to which she had reverted after the divorce. She was even less sure she wanted to discuss its legality with her daughter. She was tired of discussion. She was tired of looking for a job. She was tired of rejection and failure at every turn.

"It doesn't matter, anyway. I'm not sure I want the job. Besides, there may be other things lined up for me."

That wasn't entirely true. The letters she had sent out had not produced any results so far. But Chrissie didn't know that.

"Look for something else if you want, Mom, but apply for this one, too. Don't you see? It's not about a job. It's about getting you off your butt and on with your life!"

"Christine Wilt Gard! Don't you dare talk to your mother that way!"

"I'm sorry, Mom. But you can't continue like this. Even Helen's been saying how unhappy you look— despite your snazzy haircut. You need to start living your life again, and I think a job… No, not *a* job, *this* job. I think it just might do it."

"But, Chrissie—"

Her daughter ignored her. "Do you remember when I wanted to be on the track team?"

"Yes, Chrissie, of course I remember. That was the highlight of tenth grade, maybe even of high school for you," Lauren said, her fatigue and resignation evaporating as she recalled her daughter's determination. "I don't think anyone wanted anything so badly or tried so hard."

"And remember how every one told me I would never make it? I wasn't fast enough. I wasn't athletic enough." She paused, long enough for Lauren's memories of the time to fully return. "Do you know why I bothered to try?"

"Because you were a determined, stubborn girl with a winning streak who grew up to be a determined, stubborn young woman who doesn't know when to give up on her mother."

Chrissie laughed, and Lauren could feel a warm glow spread through her. She wasn't prepared for what came next.

"It was because of you, Mom."

"Because of me? Chrissie, I—"

"Because you were the only one who didn't tell me not to."

Lauren couldn't think of anything to say. Once again silence filled the air.

"The funny thing is, when I think back, I'm pretty sure you didn't think I'd make it, either," Chrissie went on. "So why didn't you say something?"

Chrissie had been a frail child. She had been born early, at eight months and had spent her first three months under close medical observation. She had her usual share of childhood illnesses, and Lauren tried very hard not to coddle her more than she had Jeff, who was stronger, less vulnerable and more athletic from the start. Then, at nine, Chrissie had a very bad bout with pneumonia that nearly scarred one of her lungs.

Although the pediatrician recommended exercise—including running—to strengthen Chrissie's respiratory capacity, no one thought the girl would ever be able to compete with other, healthier children. Throughout grade school and junior high, she was consigned to the sidelines.

It came as a big surprise when, in tenth grade, Chrissie announced her desire to join the track team. No one believed she would make it. Not even Lauren. Unlike everyone else, however, Lauren didn't question her daughter's enthusiasm. She swallowed her disbelief and allowed Chrissie to pursue her dream.

Lauren couldn't really remember why she had done that. But she was pretty certain it had something to do with that wide-eyed wonder, that stubborn look captured in the photograph in front of her.

Now, to her daughter, she said, "Because you wanted it so much. Because it gave you something to look forward to. Because it got you out of the house every day and onto the field. Because it really didn't matter whether you made the team or not."

"And I didn't."

No, she didn't. Not that time anyway. But the coach was so impressed with her efforts that he encouraged her to try again the next year. He even gave her some advice about training. The second time Chrissie tried out, she made it.

"And that's what I'm telling you now," Chrissie said. "It doesn't matter if you get that column, Mom. But you have to try. You just have to."

* * *

"Do you have anything for me from Thomas Bailey?" Clare asked her assistant on her way into her office.

"Nothing I can think of, but let me take a quick look." Anne Wright glanced quickly at her in-box and riffled through some documents. "Nope. Nothing."

"Not good," Clare said more to herself that to the other woman.

The "boys" were up to their old tricks. They obviously hadn't liked her interference in the internal job search and they weren't going to make things easy for her. But she was as much a partner as Junior, more so if her billing hours and client list were anything to go by. He had made it because of his name, she because of her effort.

Well, not entirely.

When Clare had begun at Bailey, Brooks and Kantowicz only a few years after graduating from Yale Law School, she was determined to make partner. She had worked harder than anyone. She had practically moved into her office, giving up every other part of her life. Not that she regretted those personal sacrifices. After what had happened to her in Boston, she didn't want to get burned again. Still, she was surprised to learn, not long after, that for all the big speeches about equality and equal opportunity, if you weren't one of the "boys," you were nobody.

Several years later, a former junior associate threatened to sue the firm for illegal termination of contract.

She had been having an affair with Thomas Bailey Senior—one of his many notorious in-house romances. When his wife had found out, he had ended the affair and fired the associate.

The case had never gone to court. The woman had settled instead for a hefty sum and a series of conditions. Among them: Bailey, Brooks and Kantowicz would hire a woman partner from inside the firm. Clare had been that person.

Confident that she had since risen to the occasion and proved herself deserving of the title, Clare also knew for a fact that most of the older lawyers and some of the younger ones still resented her presence. They felt strongly that she was not worth the plaque on her door. They scrutinized her every move, hoping she would slip. They didn't go so far as to sabotage her work, but they certainly didn't make it any easier. Thomas Junior, who acted as if the firm were his private kingdom, was one of the worst offenders. Withholding the list of internal candidates to take over the Van Belden account was not the worst trick he'd played.

Junior must have a lot of time on his hands to pull such sophomoric antics, Clare thought with a sigh.

Realizing Anne was waiting for her, she said, "Do you think you could talk to his assistant and get that shortlist we talked about?"

Some time later, Anne returned with the list in hand. Clare thanked her. She leaned back in her chair, examining it closely for promising women associates. Her heart sank with a loud thump when she spotted one name.

Anton Muller.

CHAPTER 5

Lauren folded the newspaper and threw it on the recycling pile in the corner of the room. Funny how just going through the Wanted ads gave her a routine and a sense of accomplishment. Just as writing the application to the *Chicago Gazette* had.

After her conversation with Chrissie, Lauren had decided to give the position a go. She'd tinkered with her résumé, deleting anything that might reveal who she really was and how much she had actually published. She wasn't lying, she reminded herself, taking her cue from her friends. People embellish their résumés all the time. They omit elements when necessary, tailoring them for a specific job. And if the *Gazette* really was interested, she'd tell them the truth. She had no problem with giving her age and her name.

Once Lauren had sent the letter, she hadn't given it too much thought.

Well, not exactly.

She had wondered what her chances were. She had speculated whether her tone was too dark and dismal.

After a week, she had imagined her letter in the reject pile. Now, after ten days, she considered whether it was once again time to face defeat. She was becoming quite good at that. It didn't even hurt too much. Maybe there was something to be said for that.

Lauren shrugged and glanced at the stack of newspapers on the floor. She really should put them out for recycling. But there was time. It wasn't as if anybody else cared how long they remained and what kind of a mess they made. Helen certainly didn't.

The younger woman had yet to adjust to her new residence and to the order Lauren sought to impose. Small wonder she was always searching for something missing!

That is, when she wasn't preoccupied with her wardrobe. To Lauren's bemusement, Helen continued to experiment with her clothes. In the past ten days, she had gone through the conservative two-piece uptown fashion, the bohemian look of a flowing dress worn over jeans, and the sixties retro style, which included a garish orange-and-purple dress that Lauren wouldn't have considered in her worst nightmare. Lauren wondered what was coming next. She sincerely hoped it wouldn't be punk—with spiky purple hair and pierced eyebrows. But then, it could hardly be more outrageous than anything else Helen had attempted.

If only Helen tried as hard to keep the place as she found it.

In the meantime, Helen's abandoned scarves and

discarded shoes cluttered the space as much as her misplaced books, notebooks and computer disks. More and more annoyed, Lauren wasn't sure what to do about it.

"I've dropped all the hints I can," she had told Alice Mirosek the last time they spoke.

"Maybe you need to be more straightforward about it."

"Maybe." Lauren wasn't sure it was worth the hurt feelings and the animosity.

"So was Frank interested in that lecture at the Art Institute?" she asked, changing the subject to her friend's latest efforts with her husband.

Alice groaned and reported that he had agreed to go, but only if they would be back in time to watch the season finale of his favorite reality television show.

Maybe she should throw Frank and Helen together and have them deal with the reality of this mess, Lauren now thought, her gaze wandering back to the stack of papers on the floor. She really needed to do something about it.

Funny how after taking the old papers to the bin in front of the house for more than a year, she still fought the urge to do it. She expected Charles to saunter into the breakfast room, tilt his head toward the corner and, with his crooked smile, ask her if he should remove them. It was one of the few things he had done around the house, one of the little rituals from their years together, unacknowledged when it occurred, but missed now that it didn't.

No point in missing it any longer, Lauren thought, working harder than usual at swallowing a lump in her throat. With angry determination, she bundled the stack and carried it out.

The phone was ringing when Lauren stepped back inside. She picked it up, expecting Clare or Alice or Chrissie. She hadn't spoken with any of them for a while.

"Ms. Wilt?" It was a voice she didn't recognize.

"Yes?"

"This is Sherelle Thomas from the *Chicago Gazette*. I'm calling about the letter you recently sent us."

"The letter?" Lauren sank into the nearest chair.

"Yes, about the column. I hope you're still interested in writing it."

"In writing it?" Lauren couldn't help repeating everything as a question even if it made her sound like an idiot. She covered the mouthpiece, took a deep breath and then spoke again. "Yes. Yes, of course I am."

"That's good. That's very good. Because you're our number one candidate, and we don't have a lot of time to continue with this search. We needed someone yesterday."

Lauren laughed nervously. She didn't know if she was expected to say anything. Fortunately, Sherelle continued.

"The ideas you've outlined sound promising and original. Just the sort of comic observations we're looking for. Just the kind of thing that addresses Chicago's unique take on the single life."

"Oh?"

"Oh, yes! And, you seem to fit the personal profile we're hoping to find."

Lauren felt her heart lighten. So her age didn't matter. Chrissie had been right to encourage her to apply. Maybe she should have been upfront and told them who she was, instead of fiddling with her professional experience and hiding her identity.

"Oh, good! I was worried about that. I didn't think you would want someone who—"

"Had so few publications? On the contrary. We want someone who is relatively unknown. A fresh voice."

Lauren's heart did something funny in her chest. It sunk in dismay.

"But I have to ask you this. How old are you?"

Armed with a sudden burst of self-confidence, Lauren replied, "I thought you weren't allowed to ask that. Isn't that age discrimination? Next you'll be asking me about my race."

"I'm sorry if I've offended you, Ms. Wilt, but you must understand that these are special circumstances. The column covers the single life of twenty- and thirty-year-olds, and we want a strong voice that speaks from personal experience. You have that, but something in your letter leads me to wonder whether you are not much older. Surely you—"

"I would hardly have applied if I didn't fit the criteria," Lauren said, not sure whether she was more amazed with her audacity or with her bluff.

"You may not have known them." Sherelle paused. She continued in a different tone. "But I guess we don't need to worry about it. So, do you think you can start straight away?"

"Straight away? But... But..." Lauren said, once again aware how stupid she must sound, but unable to go on.

"I'm sorry, Ms. Wilt. But as I believe I mentioned, we need some new copy immediately. Ever since our regular columnist took some unexpected unpaid leave, we've been running old columns, but we can't continue this way." Sherelle made a loud, huffing sound. Lauren could almost see her shake her head with impatience. "Are you interested and available?"

Lauren fingered her spiky hair, as if the trendy haircut would give her more courage. She didn't realize several minutes had gone by until Sherelle spoke again.

"Ms. Wilt? Are you there? Ms. Wilt?"

Okay, so maybe the *Chicago Gazette* wouldn't need to know her age to eliminate her from the pool of candidates. Maybe her general idiocy would do it.

Not if she could do something about it.

"Sorry! I'm hyperventilating with amazement here," Lauren said, unable to control the breathiness of her voice. She knew her anxiety had more to do with what she wasn't saying than with the challenge she was being offered. But that didn't stop her from hoping she sounded eager and enthusiastic, like a novice ready to combat the dragons of her first job. "Yes, of course, I'm interested and available and raring to go!"

"Great! Fantastic! I'll be expecting your material next week. E-mail it to me."

Sherelle gave her the details and briefly went through some other items Lauren would need to know to write her first column. Only after she hung up did Lauren fully acknowledge the enormity of what she had just agreed to do.

It was one thing to pretend to be under thirty when agreeing to write a column. It was another thing altogether, Lauren realized several days later, to actually write a column about the experiences of people who are twenty or thirty years younger.

What did she actually know about them, anyway? She didn't even know what her own children were up to. She had seen a lot of Chrissie since the divorce, but the two of them had spent all their time discussing Lauren. Come to think of it, she didn't even know whether Chrissie was still going out with that boy she had brought home about the time Charles had walked out. Lauren had never managed to muster any interest in him. His name escaped her now. Were he and Chrissie still together? If so, how were they managing with her move to Vienna? Lauren had to catch up as soon as she could.

But first, she had to investigate the Greater Chicago singles scene. The younger singles scene, she reminded herself, because although she had applied with her three-decade-old experience in mind, she was less and less sure that it would pass muster. Besides, Sherelle had made it clear that anything less than authentic accounts of youth life in the vast urban sprawl were not welcome.

So where could she begin? Chrissie, of course. She had got her into this mess. She could get her out of it.

But Chrissie was in Vienna, and although there were young, single people there, it could be nothing like here. Chrissie's current experience had to be distinctly different from anything the *Chicago Gazette* reader might recognize.

Chrissie, then, was out, and Jeff had never been one to confide in her—something to do with his male genes, she suspected. Anyway, after living on the West Coast for six years, he was probably as out of touch with the Chicago single scene as she was.

That left no one. Well, not exactly. Lauren could always seek inspiration from Alice's attempts to rekindle her husband's interest. But they weren't exactly young—or single, for that matter.

Of course, there was always Helen, who was certainly single and living in Chicago. But, somehow, Lauren didn't think Helen's experiences were any more representative than Chrissie's.

Then again, maybe they were. Hadn't Helen mentioned something about a dating seminar? Hadn't she wanted to write a profile for an online site? Lauren would have to look into that.

And if Helen couldn't help her? Well, then Lauren would go on her own dates. Chrissie had been trying to hook her up with someone for ages, as had several other friends. In fact, only recently, her literary agent had mentioned another writer who was very keen to meet her. Lauren had declined, with the excuse that she really wasn't interested in dating. But to keep her house, it might be worth it. It was just research, after all, and she had always been good at that.

Things weren't going the way Helen Matter had hoped.

It was more than two weeks since she had moved in with Lauren Wilt. More than two weeks since she had set out to give herself a new life, but she was still very much stuck in the old one.

Not that she hadn't tried. She had gone to one of the large commercial bookstores for how-to manuals and self-help books: How to dress, how to flirt, how to know if he is interested, how to know when not to look interested, how to get from the first date to the fourth date, and so on until you had marriage and a baby in a carriage. Then, there were a whole lot of other how-tos she didn't even want to contemplate.

Helen had studied those manuals and attended

workshops with as much diligence as when she prepared for her graduate seminars. She had thought it wouldn't be complicated, just a piece of cake, really.

Not!

The more she knew about it, the more complicated it became. Like the fact that you shouldn't fold your arms over your chest when you were at a mixer because it signaled that you weren't open and available. But you shouldn't stand with your hands down by your sides either, because that might mean you were completely lost. You shouldn't clasp them in front of you—or behind you—because that could suggest you were uptight. No one wanted to date an uptight person.

So what were you supposed to do with your hands? Helen wasn't sure. That was only one of many things she didn't know.

The one thing she did know was that she didn't stand a chance. She would have given up on this whole business if it hadn't been for Lauren.

Not that she had ever discussed it with Lauren. She had tried once, but Lauren had stared at her with that vacant look on her face, the expression people usually had when Helen told them the title of her doctoral thesis or when she described her favorite algorithmic functions, the kind that told her they didn't really understand what she was saying and they weren't going to try.

So, no, Lauren really wasn't interested in Helen's dating difficulties. Which made sense because Lauren had enough of her own difficulties, like keeping her house and finding a job. The rejections kept coming, but she went on, trying and trying. Given that, how could Helen give up on her much more humble objectives? So she, too, went on trying.

Curiously enough, Lauren seemed aware of that. The last few days, she seemed more interested. Helen had caught her reading information brochures from one of the dating workshops she had attended. Lauren had asked why Helen thought she needed to go to something like that and whether she really got anything out of it. Another time, when Helen had mentioned online dating, Lauren wanted to see the site. They had spent quite a bit of time together speculating about whether or not the descriptions were reliable or if some PR person had drawn them up. Helen wondered whether Lauren was interested in writing up personal descriptions for people who really had no talent at communication. There couldn't be too much money in that.

They had also started discussing Helen's dates. Not that there had been many. Only three since she had moved in, and all catastrophes. Helen hadn't even needed to sit down at the restaurant table to exclude the first guy. Her second date was slightly more promising, until he opened his mouth. She had a hard time spending the rest of the evening, let alone the rest of her life, with someone who made Josh sound riveting by comparison. The third guy might have been okay, except that he was a mathematician—something the friend who had set up the date forgot to mention. There was no way Helen was going close to one of those again.

Lauren had laughed sympathetically when Helen had recited her misadventures. But there had been something a bit off about her voice. Something that sounded less like interest and more like curiosity. A very special kind of curiosity. So Helen had finally asked, "Are you thinking of going on one yourself? I could help you. I mean, if you want to. I know someone who—"

"That's okay, Helen. It's very kind of you, but don't worry about it. Actually, I, um, am going on one. Chrissie set it up."

So if Lauren was still trying, despite everything she had been through, surely Helen could just keep on trying as well.

"Now, I know where Chrissie gets her good looks," Andrew Rose said, his right hand taking Lauren's in his firm clasp while his left hand moved to the small of her back and guided her toward a free table.

Lauren fought hard against the urge to roll her eyes and retort, "Oh? I didn't know you had met her father."

Instead, she accepted the compliment, offering what she hoped looked like a demure but grateful smile, allowing him to direct her across the room. She reminded herself that it was all for a good cause, but that didn't stop her from cursing Chrissie for arranging this ordeal.

She would have thought that after all these years of Ms and *Cosmo*, *Oprah* and *Sex and the City*, men would have worked on better lines. Instead it was same old, same old, and judging by Andrew, it was very old! Contrary to popular opinion and the dating industry, things hadn't changed all that much from her distant past. At least where dating was concerned.

Which was why *she* hadn't been looking forward to tonight. Chrissie was another story.

"I'm so glad you're finally going to meet him, Mom," her daughter had said, her excitement tangible over the phone. "He was my favorite professor, and I know you'll like him. You have so much in common."

Lauren couldn't imagine what she had in common with a fifty-five-year-old law professor, except their age and maybe her daughter. Oh, and that they were both divorced. That had been the main topic of conversation during her last date, eight months ago. She really didn't want to have it again.

Still, she did need to do some research for her column. Although she had gleaned some information from Helen, there was nothing like hands-on experience. Even if the thought of going on a blind date again made her skin crawl.

Now, as she waited for the waitress to bring their orders and as she chitchatted with her daughter's college idol, Lauren's revulsion came back, making her understand and even sympathize all the more with what she had deemed Helen's far too quick dismissal of her blind dates.

She tried to think of one good reason why she should give Andrew a sporting chance. For all his familiarity with international human rights law, he hadn't caught up with the times. He ordered wine for her, intercepting the waitress before Lauren had a chance to examine the menu. If he thought he was just being old-fashioned and gentlemanly, then how did he explain the flirtatious smile he exchanged with the waitress? And the extra moment his eyes lingered on her cellulite-free behind? Didn't he realize she was younger than Chrissie?

After that, Lauren found it a little hard to take him seriously. The evening went from bad to worse, as the conversation started and stalled more times than she did when plagued by writer's block. Somehow, Andrew always managed to bring it back to himself. A question about her book project veered into the difficulty he was having finding a publisher for his scholarly tome. An observation about the wine developed into a lengthy travelogue of his recent trip to Italy.

Of course, Andrew was interested in other people. It was just that most of them were in much better shape than she was. She stopped counting the times his eyes followed a curvaceous blonde or a leggy redhead, inevitably more than a decade younger than she was—and at least twenty pounds lighter. If her readers were going to be as tough on her as Andrew was, she would never stand a chance with her column.

"I can't tell you how grateful Chrissie is for your help in getting her this position," Lauren said, in an umpteenth attempt to have a two-way conversation. "Mind you, I would have preferred it if she'd stayed a bit closer to home."

"Chrissie is such a promising wo…uh, lawyer," Andrew said.

Lauren gave him a closer look. Had Chrissie pushed her into some giant misunderstanding, or was she the only one who was getting her wires crossed?

As she listened to Andrew Ross exalt Chrissie's fine mind and outstanding intelligence, Lauren felt more and more like a prospective mother-in-law inspecting her daughter's fiancé than a woman on a blind date. Ordinarily, she would have enjoyed hearing about her wonderful daughter. But tonight was supposed to have been her night of fun, even if she really expected nothing more from Andrew than some ideas for her column. But it seemed that older women such as she stood no better chance on the dating scene than they did in the teaching and singles world. Everyone wanted the younger face and the fresher attitude and the firmer body.

All of a sudden, it just didn't seem worth a minute longer of her time. If this was what the dating scene had to offer, she would rather remain single.

As if she had any choice in the matter, she thought,

noticing Andrew's eyes wander yet again toward a thirty-something in high heels and a very short skirt.

"Gosh, I didn't realize how late it was." Lauren stood up to leave. "I really must get going. It's been nice meeting you, Andrew. I'm sure Chrissie will be pleased to hear we finally met."

She was relieved Andrew didn't suggest anything else, but later, as she entered her home, she realized she had come away empty-handed in more ways than one. No man. No material for her column. She was going to have to do some serious undercover investigating soon, but it was too late for her first column.

What on earth could she write for tomorrow?

CHAPTER 6

I can do this.

Lauren waited for her computer to boot up. The tiny light in the center of the screen started to blink. The hard disk whirred and whizzed into action. Lauren focused on what she could write. Contrary to her computer, her brain was shutting down.

Last night's date had put a real damper on her determination. Only the thought of losing the house and Chrissie's respect had forced her out of bed and into her office this early. Still, she wasn't sure it would be enough to meet her end-of-the-day deadline. If she didn't have something done in the next three hours, she would have to kiss the column goodbye. Surely, it was worth a try.

She took a deep breath, then pulled out her idea pad. Not one of her jottings spoke to her now, not one was sufficiently attention-grabbing for the first column.

What was I thinking? She ignored Chrissie's bold and encouraging smile in the framed photograph and tried to get up. In spite of herself, she stayed seated in front of the illuminated screen.

I'm single, I can write, I can do this. Her hand on the mouse, she opened a new blank document.

She glanced up over the screen. A discolored corner of the wall where she had once displayed a portrait of her happy family caught her attention.

I was married for almost thirty years. I have two adult children. What do I know about the single life? Without typing a word, she closed the document and attempted to push herself off the chair and away from the screen.

Again some large force held her down.

My kids have flown the coop. I've been divorced for more than a year. I've been on a few blind dates. I can do this. She opened a new blank document, positioned her hands on the keyboard and prepared for the first sentence.

The skin on her hands was so dry it was almost flaking. And those marks? More age spots? And those protuberances? When had she replaced her knuckles with doorknobs? She really was beginning to show her age.

What was I thinking? I'm more than twenty years too old for the *Chicago Gazette*. Come to think of it, I'm twenty years too old for the last man I dated. Twenty years too old to seek comfort in a pair of shoes—unless they're Birkenstocks or Dr. Scholl's. Twenty years too old to remember that J-Lo and Eminem are singers, not foods. And the only reason I even know all this is because of my kids—who, before I know it, will also be twenty years too old for the singles column in the *Chicago Gazette*.

Lauren's hands dropped to her side. Her feet pushed off the floor. She rolled herself back and away from the screen.

Again, the invisible force prevented her from moving.

A single woman is a single woman at any age. I can do this. She propelled herself forward and once more poised her hands over the keyboard. This time, she refused to look down at them.

What's the difference between Chrissie and me? What's the difference between Helen and me? For that matter, what's the difference between Helen and Chrissie?

And suddenly it came to her. Why obsess with the differences between youth and age? Why obsess with what she didn't know about their single experience, when the real issue was the diversity of the single state? Regardless of age.

She wasn't single by choice, but her lawyer Clare and her agent Louise were. Her houseguest Helen was redefining herself for a Mr. Right she had yet to find; and her daughter Chrissie was pursuing fame and fortune in foreign lands without a thought to marriage, while Anne, Clare's assistant, was buying matching towels for a man who didn't know how to commit.

Stop.

Why focus on the dating circuit when being single could mean so much more? Did it always have to be a stepping-stone to something else? True, Lauren wasn't exactly comfortable with all her empty hours, blank walls and solitary meals, but surely that was better than another drink with Andrew, her date from hell.

Because if there was one thing she had learned last night, it was that she could do far worse than be single. She could hook up with another self-centered man. Well, she'd been there and done that. She really didn't want a repeat. Maybe it was time to enjoy her single life. Maybe dating wasn't the only way to think of the single state.

Being single is a multiple experience—and not just where partners are concerned, Lauren typed.

Fifteen minutes later, she paused to read the words on the screen. She made a number of corrections, then let her hands drop to her sides as she pondered how to continue. Her mind flew back to her conversation with Chrissie and, once again, her hands—flaking, spotted and gnarled though they were—moved across the keyboard.

Even the census bureau acknowledges our multiple choices. Married folks have only one box, but singles can check divorced, separated or just plain old single. And that's only because the census bureau doesn't think it's politically correct to distinguish between in-the-field singles and stuck-at-home ones.

Then there is the variety of living arrangements. For couples, there's only one possibility:

the two of you and maybe the pets and kids. But singles can bunk by themselves or cohabitate with other singles. Single parents live with their kids; many older single kids take shelter with their parents.

Lauren's fingers hovered over the keyboard, waiting for her brain to speed them on. Relaxing her arms and flexing her hands, she read the screen again. She was off to a good start. She smiled, saved the document and continued to type.

Several days later, her first column in print, Lauren was still glowing over Sherelle's complimentary e-mail. Lauren was much too happy to be annoyed by the lunchtime crowd at the snack bar where she was meeting Clare, much too pleased to mind any time someone younger and better-looking nudged past her. She waited patiently for her turn, ordered a sandwich and a latte and glanced around the crowded room again.

Still no sign of Clare. No sign of an empty table either. They just might have to eat standing up. But even tired legs and a worn-out back couldn't destroy Lauren's good mood.

Fortunately, just as she was ready to give up, she spotted a newly vacated table for two. She grabbed it.

"…he call you?" one of the women at the table next to her asked.

Even if Lauren didn't want to listen, with the tables so close, she didn't have a choice. But with her next column in mind and the trio of thirty-something women at her elbows, she was eager to overhear, especially this conversation.

"No, he sent an e-mail," the brunette said, the sad look on her face mirroring her gloomy tone. "I got it this morning at work."

"So it's off?"

"Not off, but too late."

"That wouldn't have happened if you had a computer at home," a slightly plump woman enjoying a large sandwich piped in. "Don't say I didn't tell you. You gotta keep up with the times, honey, or lose out on the time of your life."

"I know what you mean," the prim-looking woman who had spoken first said with a vigorous nod. "In the old days, it used to be enough to buy a new dress, but today a girl needs to make a side trip to the nearest electronics store."

"Uh-huh. You don't hook up with a fellow anymore. The only hooking up we do is with the Internet."

"I mean what kind of a chance do you have if you haven't gone online? No dating without it, that's for sure."

"No chat rooms," the prim woman said.

"No instant messaging."

"No e-mail," the sad brunette concluded.

The other two gave her a commiserating glance.

Then they attended to their food while Lauren digested more than her sandwich.

The shrill ring of a cell phone resonated from the trio's table. Apparently, it wasn't just the Internet that had changed the life of the single girl. All three women reached into their purses. The lucky one gloated as the others continued eating.

In the old days, a woman would have needed a man in tow to achieve that proud look. Now all it took was his voice. As the Virginia Slims ad used to say, "We've come a long way, baby!"

"Good. You started without me." Clare glided into the seat. "Alice couldn't make it?"

"Something came up at work. Or so she claims," Lauren explained.

"There's a lot going on at the bank, these days," Alice had told Lauren when they'd talked earlier. "They're putting in a new system, and it's not at all what I'm used to. It gets harder and harder to learn these new tricks, doesn't it?"

"It sure does," Lauren had agreed, thinking of her own life. "Any luck with Frank?"

"Not really," Alice replied a bit too quickly. "You know, this marriage business is a lot of work, it's tiring me out. Sometimes, I wish I were single again. At least, I would have more fun. But don't worry, I'll think of something. Now, tell me—what are you thinking for the column?"

Lauren had allowed her friend to steer the conversation away from herself. Now, she wondered if she had been too easily diverted. She couldn't let Alice give up so quickly.

"Too bad," Clare said, now unwrapping her sandwich. "How have you been?"

"Busy. But I just figured out what my next column is going to be about."

"Yeah?"

"Yeah. 'Tools for the Dating Game.' Forget the Rules. What we need is a guide to high-tech dating. Complete with a how-to manual." Lauren nodded toward the three women at the next table and bent forward so only Clare could hear her. "However did we manage without answering machines and cell phones, voice mail and e-mail? And those fancy handheld thingies that keep track of dates and addresses?"

"The low-tech, old-fashioned way. A little bit of healthy flirting and a lot more direct interaction." Clare removed a pickle and set it on the discarded sandwich wrapping.

"Right. Look who's talking."

"I was thinking of you actually. I've always had a thing for gadgets." Clare wriggled her eyebrows suggestively. "You might want to give them a try."

Lauren raised her chin like a prim schoolteacher. "I'm not ready for all these devices."

"They serve their purpose."

"I'm not sure I want to hear this." Lauren pressed her hands against her ears.

Clare concentrated on her sandwich and waited for Lauren to start eating again. "I can't tell you how convenient gadgets are when it comes to breaking up."

"You mean you…" Lauren didn't finish her sentence.

"Not me. But apparently Dear John text messages are the latest in-thing."

Lauren shook her head disapprovingly. "Why bother to say anything at all?"

"That's not very civilized."

Lauren wondered about the definition of civilized, but gave all her attention to her sandwich.

"Men have been doing it for centuries," Clare mused after a while. "Technology just evens things out a bit."

"What's this? Equal opportunity in heart breaking?"

Clare had always put on a great hard-and-tough act. Listening to her, it was easy to get the impression that she thought men were toys you threw out when broken and replaced with something new and better. Yet, Lauren suspected that despite all her bravado, there wasn't a constant stream of men in Clare's life. She was not as heartless as she pretended. Besides, she was far too busy, too committed to her career to be a playgirl.

But was Clare's career enough for her? Did she ever regret not having someone to go home to, someone to cuddle with when the going got tough? Or was she tough enough on her own? Curious about someone who had pursued a path so different from her own, Lauren had asked these questions soon after she and Clare had first met. Clare had answered vaguely about a choice she had made. Blinded by her domestic contentment at the time, Lauren had thought it a very lonely choice. She couldn't imagine making it herself, no more than she could imagine a life without Charles and her children. Yet that was exactly the life she was living now. Would she be able to it? She only had to look at Clare to know it was possible.

"…is good for the goose," Clare was saying. "Of course, technology has its problems, too. Did I ever tell you about the time I pressed Redial and left a message describing the worst date of my life? Turns out it was his number." She pulled a face. "The end of a not-so-beautiful relationship."

Without waiting for Lauren's reaction, Clare continued recounting cell phone screwups. "One of my clients was harassing her ex by phone. Except she forgot to hide her number, so it flashed every time she hit Redial. That was the end of anonymity. And then there's…"

Lauren listened, noting Clare's feigned indifference as much as her humorous anecdotes. Lauren knew firsthand that Clare was anything but indifferent to the feelings of her divorcing clients. She had been Lauren's lifeline, as a lawyer and a friend. So why the act?

Lauren returned to her current obsession. "So you think technology would make a good column?"

"There's certainly enough material there, but I think you're missing something important."

"You're right. I don't have much experience with this high-tech stuff." She toyed with the discarded sandwich wrapping. "I was hoping you could help me."

"You know I'd do anything I can, but there are areas where your technical expertise exceeds mine."

"Right." Lauren scrunched the paper into a tidy bundle to be tossed away. "As in good housekeeping."

"There is that. But I'm still thinking about important tools for the single woman."

"Those self-help gadgets you mentioned earlier?" Lauren said.

"Not that." Clare waved her finger. "You renovated your house, Lauren. You are an experienced do-it-yourself person."

"Only with a whole lot of help from the carpenter, plumber and electrician."

"Of course. But that's still a lot more than most women, single or married. If there's one thing a single woman needs, it's basic instruction in home repairs."

"Now, that's funny coming from you. I'm sure you never do your own repairs. Any more than you do your own housekeeping."

"Not me. I can afford to pay someone." Clare set her sandwich down and nodded at the three women next to them. "But a lot of working women can't. One of our new paralegals was telling me how she had to pay a fortune to get her toilet to stop leaking. It took the plumber fifteen minutes, and he told her she could have done it herself."

Lauren nodded. She knew a bit about plumbing. "He's right. There are a few simple, basic things worth knowing."

"So write about them," Clare said, pressing her finger down on the table. "Columns on tech tools for dating are a dime a dozen, but skills to fix up the house, that's a whole other thing."

"It's certainly a new way of thinking about singles."

And the more she thought about it, the more Lauren liked the idea. Just because a woman was on the market for a man didn't mean she shouldn't learn to get on without him. As she listened to Clare go on about how she barely knew the difference between a Phillips and a flat-head screwdriver, Lauren was already pondering this new angle. And by the time Clare had finished her lunch, Lauren had the last line for the column.

So the next time someone asks, "What is a single girl's best friend?" don't say diamonds. Or Manolo Blahniks. Say technology. And then learn how to use it.

Clare waved goodbye to Lauren and headed back to her office. Lauren was looking so much better these days. The haircut had done something to her face, but the real change had come with the column. Writing it was obviously good for her. She was finally beginning to realize how much she still had and how much more she could still do. She was trying something new and different. Amazingly, she was actually enjoying herself.

Clare almost envied her. Not that she wasn't happy or wanted to trade in her life. She was proud of everything she'd done, especially considering where she had started. But she did wonder sometimes what it would be like if things were different, if she had a husband and children, someone to go home to, to care for, to take care of her. Someone like Anton.

She blinked rapidly, forcing herself not to think about his dark hair, blue eyes and gentle voice, telling herself nothing could come of this totally inappropriate attraction she felt for him.

It had always been there, she realized, but she'd considered it a little thing. Ever since he had seen her drunk, it seemed to have gotten stronger, as though the gentleness and the concern he had displayed that evening had changed from something purely physical into something more.

Now she practically trembled every time she thought of him. Yes, she, Clare Hanley, in her mid-forties and a senior partner at a major Chicago law firm, trembled when she thought of Anton Muller. Who would have thought?

She couldn't do anything about it, of course. His

name on the short list to take over the Van Belden account meant that any relationship between them was impossible. The office gossips would immediately claim he'd gotten the account in exchange for bedroom services. She would never be able to wipe the smirk off Bailey Jr.'s face. Worse, she would never know if that had been Anton's intention all along. A man's ambition had burned her once. She wasn't going to let it happen twice.

Of course, Anton was nothing like that other guy. But she wouldn't, she couldn't give him a chance to use her that way. Besides she didn't need to. She wasn't depressed and unhappy with her single life, like Lauren. She was quite all right alone—absolutely fine.

"Lauren? It's Sherelle Thomas here. Great column you sent last week. I just loved that line about letting our feet carry us away. I'm the kind of woman who changes boyfriends as often as shoes, although I hold on to the old pairs and let go of the men. But, girl, there might be something to keeping them at hand. Or should that be in step?" Sherelle laughed at her own joke.

Lauren sputtered softly into the phone, more out of politeness than anything else. She wondered what her editor would think if she realized how little Lauren actually knew about shoe fashion and manhunts. The idea for the column had come to her when she was grocery shopping. Between her aching feet and the pudgy men in the aisle, she had begun to fantasize. Before she knew it, she had scripted another column.

She was really getting into the hang of this business. Her first two columns had been difficult, but once she began writing things changed. She liked research best, spying on younger women, eavesdropping on their conversations and learning about their lives.

"We're getting a lot of mail for you," Sherelle said. "You need to come in and see it. Of course, I can get one of the interns to sort it for you, but readers do like personalized answers."

"Can't you mail it to me? I can go through it at home. I, um, have my own filing system."

"That is a possibility, but it would be nice to meet you finally. It's been three weeks, and I still don't know what you look like. You didn't come to the staff meeting. Or the staff party. I'm beginning to think you're avoiding us, Lauren. Don't tell me you're hiding something."

"No, I'm not hiding a—" Lauren began.

"Maybe you're a werewolf?"

"No, I'm—"

"Or worse." Sherelle made a scary sound. "A man."

"Nothing like that. I'm just a busy woman."

Lauren wondered whether Sherelle would laugh so hard if she knew the truth. In the world of trendy singles columnists, wasn't being an older woman worse than being a werewolf or a man?

"So busy you can't stop by to see us? We also need to set up a photo shoot."

"A photo shoot?"

"Yes. Market surveys tell us readers usually like a face to go with the column, and we like to give them what they want."

"I can't do a photo shoot."

"Why not?"

"I just can't. That's all."

"Do you have a disfigured face?"

"No." Not unless wrinkles and age spots counted. But then, in the fashion-conscious woman's press, age was a major disfigurement.

"Are you on a Wanted list?"

"No. Of course not." But maybe she would be if Sherelle ever found out the truth.

"Maybe you're hiding from someone."

"No, no. Nothing like that." The only person she was hiding from was on the other end of the line.

"A man maybe? Oh my God!" Sherelle inhaled loudly. "You're not married, are you?"

"No. I'm just a very private person. I don't want my picture appearing everywhere."

"You better get used to fame, then. You won't be able to go anywhere once our PR people get hold of you."

"PR?"

"Yes. They want to run a poster campaign on you.

Maybe even get you on a morning talk show. They want to make you really hot. Girl, you are going places!"

"Oh my goodness!" Lauren exclaimed. She fanned herself, hoping it would help her breathe.

Sherelle laughed again. "So about that photo shoot? When can you do it?"

There was no way Lauren could agree to that photo shoot. That would be it. The end. Without the sunset and the happily ever after. Of course, even without the photo shoot, it would be the end. And if Sherelle wanted payback, all she had to do was tell a few people in the right places. It would be the end of not just one, but two beautiful careers. Because the publishers of Lauren Gard's wholesome autobiographical essays wouldn't want anything to do with her once the truth came out about her salacious speculations on the single life.

As Lauren struggled against the waves of desperation, she remembered something.

"I need to be incognito."

"Incognito?"

"Yes, incognito. Disguised. Unknown. Anonymous."

"Oh?"

"Yes. I shouldn't tell you this, Sherelle, but that's how I get my ideas for the column," she said, relieved to be telling the truth, part of it, anyway. "I spend a lot of time in public places, listening in on conversations, like a modern-day Haroon El Rashid."

"Rashid?"

"You know, the caliph in the *One Thousand and One Nights*."

"One Night? You mean *First Knight*, don't you? But I'm sorry, you lost me."

Clearly Sherelle had a very different reading list from hers. Lauren searched for a more accessible reference, then opted for a simple explanation. "If people know who I am, they'll start to watch themselves more. And there goes my scoop. It's bad enough when my friends watch themselves."

"I had no idea!" Sherelle sighed. "I suppose you're right. Okay, no photo shoot for the moment. But you have to come in. You can hide from everyone, but you can't hide from me!"

Lauren exhaled. She had won one battle, she had to concede this one. "Okay. I'll stop by the day after tomorrow. Is that soon enough for you?"

"The day after tomorrow's good."

What had she been thinking?

Sherelle Thomas might like her ideas. She might enjoy Lauren's writing. She might even be fooled by her voice. But all it would take was one look to know about her deception. All it would take was a couple of clicks on the Internet to know about Lauren's other identity as a writer.

How had she ever thought she could pull this off? She hadn't been thinking. It was that simple. Lately, she hadn't been thinking at all. She had known her body would turn to mush when she hit fifty. Nobody had said anything about her brain. But that was happening.

She must have been delusional to think she could jump-start her life. She must have mistaken herself for Chrissie or Helen. She wasn't on the threshold of life; she was on her way out, through the back door where no one would notice.

Forget about the column; she was never going to convince anyone she was in her early thirties. Forget about her book; she was never going to write it. Forget about the house; she would never be able to keep it.

Lauren walked to the large bay windows and looked out. Her head against a pane, she fingered the wooden frames. How she had worked to create this texture on them! When she and Charles had moved to this well-off Chicago suburb, into her grandmother's house, the window frames had been rotting. Charles wanted to replace them, but Lauren preferred to preserve the old wood and the spirit of the house. However, the decay was too extensive.

Unable to find authentic replacements, she had her own window frames made. With the right finishing techniques, a carpenter had explained to her, new wood could be given the appearance of the old. Lauren learned the process from the craftsman, working in his shop, helping with the scraping and staining. She came to love the textures and the smells, the feel of the shavings under her fingers and the soft steady sounds of the plane and brush against wood. Now, as she touched the wood and traced the pattern of the grain, those sensations came back and with them memories of her home.

All that would be lost forever when she surrendered the house to someone else. Because it would take a lot more to restore *her*. She must be incredibly naive if she thought she could replace her broken parts and refinish her worn-out places to give herself a new look and a new life. She might be able to study the part. She might even be able to write it. But there was no way she could act it. Once the truth was out, Sherelle would never let Lauren continue writing the column. Lauren might as well accept it. Her short-lived masquerade was over.

CHAPTER 7

Lauren was still reeling from her latest bout of bad news when the doorbell rang. She wanted to ignore it, but whoever it was wouldn't go away. After the third ring, she got up and opened the door. Clare pushed past her, only turning to face Lauren when she was well in the house.

"I finished early tonight. For once I'm at a loose end, so I thought I'd pay you a surprise visit," she said, her voice changing suddenly as she took in Lauren's unhappy expression. She gave her a quick appraisal.

"What's going on, Lauren? I thought things were looking up now that you have the column. You'll be able to meet the taxes and bills for the house. What's the problem?" When Lauren didn't say anything, Clare became more insistent. "Come on, Lauren, snap out of it, and let your friends help you. Come, let's have some tea."

Without waiting for an answer, Clare headed for the kitchen. Lauren didn't bother to protest. She followed. Then, leaning against the wall, she watched her friend make tea.

"I think I'm going to have to sell the house, after all," Lauren announced with a calmness that amazed her.

She had thought the divorce had taught her everything about numbed emotions, but apparently she had more to learn.

Clare spun around, a half-full kettle in her hand. "What?"

"I'm going to sell—"

"I heard what you said. I just can't believe you're going to do it."

"Well, I can. I've made up my mind."

"Just like that?"

"Yes." Lauren crossed her arms across her chest and nodded. "Just like that."

"I don't understand. You have the column. What happened?"

"It didn't work out."

"I see." Clare turned back to the sink and filled the kettle with water. She turned it on, and then faced Lauren once again. "They don't like your style?"

Lauren shrugged. Clare's eyes darted back and forth, trying to read Lauren's face and body for some explanation. Then she asked, "Well, are you going to tell me or are you just going to stand there?"

"There's nothing wrong with the column. Actually, they like it, and—" She stopped, not knowing how to continue.

"And?"

"They want to promote it. Billboards. Talk shows. You name it."

"They want to…?" Clare's head lifted as she registered what Lauren had just said. "That's great! No, that's better than great, that's fantastic! We should be celebrating! We should be drinking champagne. Hell, we should be dancing in the street! What are you waiting for?"

Realizing that Lauren wasn't responding as joyfully as she was, Clare stopped and once again examined her friend for a clue. "I don't get it. This is *good* news, isn't it?"

"It would be under normal circumstances, but these aren't normal circumstances." Lauren sighed and dropped her hands to her side. "I can't do it."

The kettle whistled. Clare ignored it. "Why not? This is what you've been waiting for, isn't it?"

"It's a bit complicated." Lauren kept her eyes on the blue and white tiles around the sink. "They, um, they think I'm a thirty-year-old."

"A thirty-year-old?"

"Yes. I didn't tell them I'm over fifty." She looked down at her fingers, woven together tighter than a tapestry. "And I didn't tell you before because I knew you wouldn't approve."

"You didn't…" Clare leaned against the counter, too surprised to attend to the kettle's shrill whistle. "Oh, Lauren!"

"It just happened. I didn't get a chance to…and well,

now my editor wants me to come in. I've been stalling all this time. You know, with e-mail and Internet. I don't need to see anyone. I just need to log in every now and then. The whole thing was working, but now, my editor is insisting on meeting me. They want pictures. I can't do it."

Clare turned away for the brief moment to turn off the kettle. Then she moved closer to her friend and gave her a soothing hug. "I'm sorry, Lauren. I'd like to help you. I really would, but I just don't understand what you're saying. You're going to have to start all over again. Slowly, please."

After taking several moments to calm down, Lauren summarized the recent events as clearly as she could, explaining how she'd fast talked her way out of a column photo. When Lauren finished, Clare was silent, digesting all the information.

"As your lawyer, I don't think you would have a problem here," she said cautiously. "But as your friend, I think you should tell the truth."

"Tell the truth? Sure I can do that, and then they can fire me. I'll have to sell the house and go back to finishing my book. Trying to, anyway."

"Stop feeling sorry for yourself, Lauren. It's not over yet. If they like your column so much now, it may not matter once they find out your age and who you really are. It's not as if teen magazines are written by teenagers or women's magazines only by women. Take a chance, Lauren. The truth isn't supposed to hurt. It's supposed to set you free."

Which didn't mean it wouldn't hurt *her*, or that it would set *her* free. Lauren opened her mouth to retort, but the sound of the front door opening and shutting stopped any further discussion.

"Oh, hello! I didn't think you would be here, Lauren!" Helen smiled apologetically as she walked into the kitchen. She backtracked a bit when she saw Clare. "And I didn't know you had company."

"It's okay," Lauren answered. "We were just making a pot of tea. You know Clare Hanley, don't you? Helen Matter is one of Chrissie's friends," Lauren told Clare, hoping her astute friend would understand that the subject they had just been discussing was off-limits.

"You're living here, in Chrissie's room, right?" Clare put another mug on the tray.

"Yes. For the moment. Lauren is an even better roommate than Chrissie. She never complains when I make a mess."

"No, Lauren wouldn't," Clare muttered so that only Lauren could hear. To Helen, she said, "Come, have some tea with us."

And just like that, Clare took over as if it were her house. Tray in hand, she led them into the adjacent breakfast room. The hot, steaming cups of tea in front of them, they sat around the oaken table and made small talk.

As Lauren listened to Clare question Helen, she began to suspect her friend was up to something. Oh, Clare was very congenial. Nobody else would have seen through her act, known that she was trying to get as much information as she could out of poor, sweet Helen. Nobody else would have guessed that behind that amiable exterior, Clare was plotting some scheme.

"How's your newest computer program coming along, Helen? I'm sure Clare would really like to hear about it," Lauren said with a smile glued on her face.

But Clare would not let Lauren redirect the conversation. She didn't even wait for Helen's answer before asking: "Tell me, Helen, do you know anyone at the *Chicago Gazette?*"

"At the *Chicago Gazette?* No." Helen shook her head slowly, then stopped, her mouth open. "A friend of mine was going to design their Web site, but I think someone else was chosen."

"Helen's a computer whiz." Lauren felt she had to come to the young woman's defense. "She's getting her doctorate in mathematics, and for a hobby she sometimes writes Web-based programs. Tell Clare about the site you're working on, the one where—"

Clare ignored Lauren again and didn't wait for Helen to respond. "But you've never had any contact with anyone at the *Gazette?*"

"No," Helen answered, a puzzled expression darkening her fair face.

An Important Message from the Editors

Dear Reader,

Because you've chosen to read one of our fine novels, we'd like to say "thank you"! And, as a special way to say thank you, we're offering to send you two more novels similar to the one you are currently reading, and a surprise gift – absolutely FREE!

Please enjoy the free books and gift with our compliments...

Pam Powers

Peel off Seal and Place Inside...

We'd like to send you two free books to introduce you to our new line – Harlequin® NEXT™! These novels by acclaimed, award-winning authors are filled with stories about rediscovery and reconnection with what's important in women's lives. These are relationship novels about women redefining their dreams.

THERE'S THE LIFE YOU PLANNED. AND THERE'S WHAT COMES NEXT.

Your two books have a combined cover price $11.00 in the U.S. and $13.00 in Canada, but are yours **FREE!** We even send you a wonderful surprise gift. You can't lose

FREE BONUS GIFT!

We'll send you a wonderful surprise gift, absolutely FREE, just for giving Harlequin NEXT books a try! Don't miss out —
MAIL THE REPLY CARD TODAY!

Order online at
www.TryNextNovels.com

THE EDITOR'S "THANK YOU" FREE GIFTS INCLUDE:

▶ Two NEW Harlequin® Next™ Novels

▶ An exciting surprise gift

YES! I have placed my Editor's "thank you" Free Gifts seal in the space provided at right. Please send me 2 FREE books, and my FREE Mystery Gift. I understand that I am under no obligation to purchase anything further, as explained on the back and opposite page.

PLACE
FREE GIFTS
SEAL
HERE

▶ DETACH AND MAIL CARD TODAY! ▶

356 HDL EE35   156 HDL EE3T

FIRST NAME	LAST NAME

ADDRESS

APT.#	CITY

STATE/PROV.	ZIP/POSTAL CODE

Thank You!

(H-NXT-04/06)

The Reader Service — Here's How It Works:

"Good. That's very good!" Clare faced Lauren. "I think we may have found the solution to your problems. Helen can go in your place."

Lauren almost dropped her mug on the table. "Are you crazy?"

"Not at all. I think it's a perfect idea. She needs a place to live, you need a job. It's the perfect trade-off."

"I really don't see how you think we would be able to pull this off."

"The way I see it, there's nothing complicated about it," Clare said calmly. "All Helen has to do is go in, say hello and pick up the mail. She goes in, she comes out. No problem."

"No problem? Only a little deception! Only a photo shoot!"

Clare wrinkled her brow. "I thought you said there wasn't going to be a photo shoot."

"Not for now. But who knows what they'll think up next?"

"But you'll be long gone by then. The column over, the house taxes and bills paid."

"And if they want to see her again?"

"No problem. Send her again. It's the perfect setup." Clare smiled with satisfaction. "Failing that, you can put them off. You seem to have developed a knack at ignoring phone calls and appointments."

Lauren snorted.

"You can do this, Lauren."

"No!"

"Yes!"

"Um, Lauren?" Helen tried to speak.

"This is the craziest thing I've ever heard!"

"You are being deliberately stubborn!"

"Um, Clare?" Helen tried again.

"It won't work!"

"It'll only go wrong if you let it!"

Lauren and Clare glared at each other.

"Lauren? Clare?" Helen turned her gaze from one woman to the other in a useless bid to intercept their incensed glares.

"What?" Lauren and Clare said in unison, scowling furiously at Helen.

"I was just, um, wondering whether you were, um, talking about me?" Her eyes continued to dart nervously between them as she searched for some kind of reassurance.

"We were," Clare answered.

Helen nodded as calmly as if they were discussing the weather. "I thought so, but I didn't completely get it. Would you explain it to me? I'm sorry. I'm not very quick about some things."

"Don't worry about it." Lauren frowned at Clare. "You're not the one who's not astute!"

"*She* certainly isn't!"

Again, Clare and Lauren faced off.

"Well?" Helen waited.

Lauren pointed her finger at Clare. "Don't you dare!"

"Look! You wanted me to help you keep the house. Everything else we've tried hasn't worked. So why don't we just see what Helen thinks? She has the right to make up her own mind."

"I've already made up mine," Lauren assured her. "Don't you even think I'll change it!"

Clare made a loud inarticulate sound, then explained her plan to Helen. The young woman's face was so transparent. She could no more conceal her delight in hearing about Lauren's success than she could hide her dismay at Clare's ridiculous and untenable scheme. How on earth, Lauren wondered, did Clare think someone like Helen could act out a lie? How did she expect Helen to discuss a job she barely understood? Weren't her recent attempts at redefining herself a perfect indication of her cluelessness?

Then again, Lauren thought taking in Helen's clothing, maybe she had learned something. She was wearing jeans and a body-clinging shirt, which were appropriately casual. She also accessorized it nicely with a silver belt that hung low over her hips. She wore just enough makeup to highlight her elfin features and give her the touch of sophistication. But all that didn't mean that Clare and Lauren could send the poor girl into a den of wolves.

So it was with the deepest regret that Lauren heard Helen say, "I'll do it. Of course, I'll do it."

Lauren pounded her fists against the table, but the other two women ignored her.

"Great," Clare said to Helen. "Now let's get you ready for that encounter. It's the day after tomorrow, so we don't have much time. But don't worry. I'm sure you can pull it off."

2414. 2415. 2416. Helen read the door numbers and cursed out loud. She was walking in circles, back where she had started ten minutes ago when she had stepped off the elevator. You would think that someone who could solve difficult algorithmic problems and design complicated computer programs could figure a way through the hallways of a building. But you would be wrong.

She had tried to concentrate when the receptionist had given her the instructions to get to Sherelle Thomas's office. But her nerves had been in overdrive. Despite her best efforts, she had tuned out. Lauren and Clare were going to be sorry they ever asked for her help. And to think that Lauren had actually worried about her.

"Are you sure you want to do this?" Lauren had asked her as they had parted company this morning. "It's not too late to pull out if you want to. You can keep the room, you know. Even if you don't do this for me."

"Oh my God, Lauren, you're so sweet. But I'm good for this. Really I am. I want to do it. Almost as much for you as for me."

Helen had meant it. This could be her chance for adventure, her chance to be someone else. Lara Croft. Carrie Bradshaw. Anyone but Helen Matter, computer geek extraordinaire who knew more about joysticks than the joy of love and life.

She took a deep breath and considered her options. There were only two: go forward or go back, or through that door on the left that might lead to something unexpected.

"Can I help you?"

Surprised, Helen whirled around, forgetting that she had traded her sneakers for heels. She swerved unsteadily, but managed to catch herself before she fell.

On surer footing, she examined the body that went with the voice. What she saw took her breath away. And then it made her want to turn around and run, down the hall, down the stairs, out of the building all the way back to Lauren's house.

He was tall and lean, with a body that told her he had not spent his entire life hunched over textbooks or a computer screen. She would have looked longer at the body, but her eyes were drawn upward, to his face. With his dark eyes, bright smile and dark, wavy hair, he had to be a male model. One of those marble-faced men she sometimes saw on the covers of glossy magazines, the kind of man who would never attend a workshop on dating—he already had everything it took.

"Can I help you?" Coverboy asked again, apparently

indifferent to her staring. After all, he made a profession of being stared at, no doubt.

Helen turned around to see if he were addressing someone else. There was no one.

"I meant you," he said, a bemused expression on his face. She pointed at herself, and he nodded, a smile creasing his face with dimples. "You look a little lost. Unless you like walking around in circles. I saw you go by here a couple of minutes ago."

Helen didn't know if she should be flattered or mortified because he had noticed her…and perhaps noted what a loser she was.

She shifted her weight and almost stumbled again. The graceless shuffle reminded her who she was supposed to be: Lauren Wilt, not a geeky bore who cowered in front of Coverboys, but a sassy, upbeat journalist who was better than the Mounties at getting her man. Forget Lara Croft. Forget Carrie Bradshaw. She was Lauren Wilt, the woman to save the day: self-confident and ready for battle.

With a graceful movement of her hand, Helen brushed back her hair, pushing it behind her shoulder with a gesture she had perfected under Clare's watchful eye. She tilted her head in what she hoped was a flirtatious gesture and met Coverboy's gaze straight-on.

"I'm looking for Sherelle Thomas's office," she said, doing her best to replicate some mixture of Melanie Griffith's little-girl voice and Drew Barrymore's breathy one.

On her, it sounded like a croak. She cleared her throat and tried again. "Sherelle Thomas. You probably don't…"

"Sherelle? Sure. I'm going that way. It's kind of tricky, if you miss this door." He pointed to the door she had contemplated what seemed a lifetime ago.

"Tricky? Now you mention it, I was expecting a white rabbit to come out with a key and point the way."

Geek. Dweeb. Nerd. If you can't be witty, don't bother to try. Just shut up. Silence is golden.

She looked at him expecting an expression of disgust. He was smiling.

"A key? I always thought it was a clock."

"That, too. I'm late."

He smiled. "Like Alice's rabbit."

Well, what d'ya know? Coverboy was actually literate. Or maybe, like her, he'd just seen the Disney cartoon. It didn't matter. With a smile like that, he didn't have to read or watch or think. He didn't have to do anything. She would do it for him. Just show her the way.

To her surprise, he did.

Well, actually, he just pulled the door open and followed her through.

"You must be Lauren Wilt. I've read your columns. They're, um…"

"That's okay. You don't have to say you like them. They're for women anyway."

"If I were a woman, I would like them. But I'm not."

Hallelujah to that! He smiled again, and Helen

knew that even Lauren would forgive him for not liking the column.

"I'm Joe, by the way. Joe Bardet. I design Web pages."

"Web pages?" Helen wobbled so much on her heels she almost sprained her ankle.

"Yeah. I'm going to be doing your pages, too."

"*You're* going to be setting up *my* pages?"

That was a first! But today she was Lauren. Lauren Wilt, creator of the *Chicago Gazette*'s "Single Life" column.

"Yeah," he said. "Didn't Sherelle tell you?"

"No." Maybe she had told Lauren, the real one, the one who had forgotten to tell her.

"That's okay." His hands moved through the air to show how little it mattered, and everything was forgotten. "She'll tell you about it now, I'm sure. Here she is."

He ushered her into an office and followed her in.

"Lauren! Come in! How nice to finally put a face to a name!"

Sherelle looked just like Helen thought an editor of a newspaper's women's pages should look: young, pretty, impeccably dressed in stylish clothes and daringly coiffed in braids. Her dark eyes sparkled with intelligence, her flawless features gleamed with energy, her whole body in tune with whatever rhythm currently held the world in sway. She was the kind of woman Helen had spent her whole life envying and despising, the kind of woman she could never hope to be. Coverboy and Sherelle would make the perfect pair, role models for the young, beautiful professionals of the day.

"You're exactly what I expected," Sherelle said, moving from behind her desk. Her eyes quickly swept over Helen's attire, taking in the short skirt and the body-fitting top that Lauren had convinced her to wear. No doubt to how she was being judged; clothes did make the woman, after all. Next time, Clare and Lauren could just send the wardrobe, forget what lay inside.

"I see you've already met Joe."

"Um, yes. I was lost. He showed me the way."

"That's good. Because you're probably going to be working together a lot."

"He mentioned—" Helen began, but Sherelle cut her short, with a toss of her braided hair.

"So, have you thought what you are going to do about your mail?"

"Um, answer it?"

Sherelle gave her a funny look. "I mean *how* are you going to answer it."

"We, um, I haven't…"

This time, Sherelle interrupted with a wave of her hands. "Some will have to be answered privately, and I'm sure there will also be a lot of material that you could use for the column. But what I really want you to consider is something interactive."

"Interactive?"

"Yes. Interactive and online. That's why Joe is here."

Of course, Helen knew what interactive meant. She'd operated her share of bulletin boards and blogs while Sherelle was working hard at perfecting that prom queen look. But Helen had no idea what Lauren would think of the idea. It hadn't entered their discussion.

"It seems—"

Once again, Sherelle cut her off. She held up her finger. "Don't say no. Think about it. It would be good PR for someone who doesn't want her face splashed around the city."

"Interactive?" Helen repeated, as if she were still trying to understand what it meant. "Wouldn't that be very complicated?"

"It's not complicated at all," Joe said, going on to briefly describe what was involved. Helen listened patiently, realizing she could probably give him some tips. He didn't seem to know about the most recent beta version of TalkSpinner, which had been designed with this kind of multiparty, real-time interaction in mind.

Helen Matter would have loved to exchange tips, files, protocols, beta versions, you name it with Joe. Lauren Wilt, however, didn't know a thing about it. So, instead of showing him a glimpse of her real gray matter, Helen tilted her head in Ally McBeal style. It was harder than she expected because she couldn't keep her eyes off Joe. All the time she was looking at him, all she could think about was how he would look up close and personal, his lips pressed against her mouth, his hands against her back.

As if. She'd had no luck with Josh and What's-His-Name from the dating service. Coverboy wasn't going to give her the time of day. But she really should listen to him. Concentrate Helen, concentrate, he's talking about computers, she told herself.

"That's all there is to it," Joe concluded with a smile.

Helen's legs wobbled for reasons that had nothing to do with her high heels. She flashed him a Julia Roberts smile.

"So, what do you think?" Sherelle asked.

"I don't know. I'm not sure about this. Do I have to decide now?"

The easiest answer of them all because there was no way she was going to get any more involved. The rest was for the real Lauren to tackle.

Fortunately, Sherelle didn't press the point. "So let's go take a look at those letters," she said. "Joe, you don't need to tag a long."

"I guess not. It was nice meeting you, Lauren. Oh, and here's my e-mail. If you want to ask me any more questions about the Web site." He handed her his card.

His long fingers skimmed hers lightly, so lightly she barely felt them, but the touch still sent tingles to the ends of her toes. She was quivering so much she could barely nod goodbye.

Helen wondered whether Sherelle could hear the

inward sigh she let out when Joe left. If so, she didn't say anything. Instead, she pointed to an adjoining room. Before she crossed over, she reached for something on her desk. "Oh, and here's an invitation to a hot new club. You might want to check it out. For your column, of course."

"Of course."

CHAPTER 8

Lauren spoke softly across the table at the Green Factory, so that only her friends could hear her, but her voice was firm. "I don't know about the Web site. It might get really complicated, and I'm not sure I want to do this to you."

Helen opened her mouth to protest, but Lauren gave her a look to show the discussion was over. "I'll have to think about it."

"And the club?" Helen asked. "Will you go?"

"I don't know."

"I'll go if you'll go," Alice said to Lauren. "Beats staying at home and competing with Frank's television shows."

"Maybe you and Frank could go," Lauren suggested. "It's just his scene, isn't it?"

Alice humphed. "It was. I think he prefers *Jeopardy* these days. I suppose I could ask. Then again, we could just have a girls' night out."

"So I guess that means I have to go," Lauren said, smiling at her friend's cherubic face.

"You'll go where?" Clare asked, not bothering to

apologize for being the last to arrive. She threw herself in the remaining chair and reached for the menu Lauren had just put down. "C'mon. Fill me in. Where are we going?"

"Nowhere, for the moment, but Lauren might be going to a club," Alice answered, setting her menu back on the table.

After the waiter had taken their orders, Clare turned to Lauren. "Well?"

"Sherelle Thomas gave Helen an invitation to that new club, The Watering Hole. Sherelle thought I could check it out and maybe do something for the column. The Smores are playing."

Clare shook her head. "The Smores?"

"The musical phenomena of this generation. If the *Chicago Gazette* is anything to go by," Lauren said. "But don't worry. I haven't heard of them, either."

"Doesn't mean anything. You haven't heard of any band since The Pretenders."

The ever-diplomatic Alice turned to the one person whose opinion about the current music scene meant something. "Have you heard of them, Helen?"

"Yes. They're, um, good. They have a great lead female singer. She, um, kind of reminds me of Chrissie Hynde."

Chrissie must have told Helen about Lauren's uncharacteristic liking for the rock star. Usually more a jazz and blues fan, Lauren had heard "Middle of the Road"

over the radio when she was thirty. The timely reso-
nance had spurred her to learn everything about the
singer who had left Akron for London. When, later,
Lauren too began to go places, she attributed her determination to finish and publish her first manuscript to
the singer's autobiographical lyrics. In honor of that, she
had taken to calling her daughter Christine, Chrissie.

Now, Lauren closed her eyes and tried to imagine
what a Chrissie Hynde of today might sound like,
but she couldn't pull it off. "As long as it's not that
horrible electronic music. The kind that sounds as if
it's squeezed through an underpowered computer," she
said, hoping that Helen's musical taste went in very
different directions.

Clare nodded. "Or the exclusive base beat of techno,
the kind that blows your ears out."

"Or that misogynistic stuff they play nonstop on the
radio," Alice added.

Lauren sipped her drink. "You realize that's pretty
much all current music."

"Not true," Clare said. "Most rock music isn't all
that different from the stuff we listened to twenty or
thirty years ago. Sometimes it's even the same musi-
cians. Mark Knopfler without Dire Straits. Phil Collins
without Genesis."

"Chrissie Hynde without The Pretenders," Lauren
added. She had a generous helping of the bread and red
pepper dip the waiter had just brought as a starter.

"Which brings us back to The Smores," Alice said. "So, you'll go?"

"I don't know," Lauren replied. "I'm not sure it's my kind of place. What would I be doing with all those kids? I mean, can you imagine if my mother had shown up at a concert at the Aragon or the Metro? I would have died." At the thought of her mother showing up anywhere near a rock music venue, Lauren burst out laughing and almost choked on the crumbs in her mouth. Alice saw the humor, too, and joined her. Clare and Helen stared at them.

"I'm sorry, Helen, Clare," Lauren said, once the giggling stopped. "But you didn't know my mother. Think Nancy Reagan. Think Queen Elizabeth."

"Not Queen Elizabeth." Alice tried very hard to keep her face straight. "At least she went to a concert in her own palace."

"Yeah, but she had earplugs in. And she certainly didn't wriggle that royal behind," Lauren said, and she and Alice yielded to more giggles. "Don't laugh. That's what they'll be saying about us if we go to this thing."

"Nah! There's nothing royal about my behind."

"And there is with mine?" Lauren lifted her eyebrows. "Seriously, Alice—"

"Seriously? I think you shouldn't confuse our generation with our mothers'," Alice said. "We're nothing like them. Can you imagine my mother wearing a skirt as short as mine when she turned fifty? She was frumpy, frilly and flowery all the way. She only wore long pleated skirts that made her hips look even wider than they were."

"She wore those even before she turned fifty," Lauren said.

"My point exactly. Look, all I'm saying is that women our age are so much cooler than our mothers were. We take care of ourselves because we know that life isn't over. We eat better, dress better, look better. Think of all the amazing-looking fifty-year-olds around today."

"Name one."

"Besides myself?"

Lauren huffed loudly. "Besides yourself. And Clare. Who's a real looker in that short skirt and those red sandals. But she's not yet fifty, so she doesn't count."

"Susan Sarandon."

Surprised, everyone looked at Helen.

"I hope I look like her one day," the young woman went on. "In fact, I'd be happy to look like her now."

"Good point." Alice nodded. "Goldie Hawn—almost as attractive as her twenty-something daughter. Rose-anne Carter, with a new album that's probably better than anything the yung'uns ever did. You should see the way Frank drools over her." She rolled her eyes. "About the only thing that has him drooling these days."

"You should be happy about that," Lauren said. "Doesn't drooling come with the seventh age of man? The last one? At least he's got a few more ages to go through."

"You know, *that* is not what I meant. And don't try to change the subject. What do all those women have that you don't?"

"A little plastic surgery?"

Alice frowned. "I don't think so. Besides who's going to notice plastic surgery in the dark."

"In the dark?"

"Yes. Lights are down and low at rock concerts. Remember? Don't tell me you have Alzheimer's as well."

"Must've forgot," Lauren quipped.

But she didn't laugh. Her attention was fixed on a couple who had just entered the room: a man who carried himself with supreme self-assurance and a woman who looked like she still believed one day it would all be hers.

"Hello, Charles. Hello, Tracie," Lauren said as the couple stopped at their table. She hoped she sounded more composed than she felt. Of all the places she could have run into Charles, she never imagined The Green Factory. He was such a carnivore; he'd never appreciated her experimentation with vegetarian cuisine. Neither had Chrissie. Only Jeff had taken to it.

"Hello, Lauren. It's good to see you."

"Likewise. You should have come a bit earlier. There were more tables."

"That's okay. We have reservations."

They would. Just because Charles no longer had Lauren to take care of his life for him didn't mean he hadn't found someone else.

"Well, you'd better hurry along, then. They'll be giving it away."

Charles looked as if he wanted to say something, but instead just nodded and let Tracie lead him away.

She contemplated his back briefly, trying to ignore the tightening of her chest and the sinking feeling in her stomach. She was relieved that her friends were chatting on without her. She wasn't capable of saying a word. Despite the year that had gone by, it still hurt to see him. It still hurt that he had thrown away the life they had built together for someone not much older than his daughter. What was it about youth that made it so desirable to some men?

Lauren turned to the other women at the table. Ignoring the concerned looks they were giving her, she smiled extra brightly. "Okay. I'll do it. I'll go to the club."

Clare high-fived Alice. "All right!"

"There's one slight problem," Lauren said.

The three other women looked at each other. "Name it," Alice said. "We'll take care of it."

Lauren pointed at Clare and Alice. "You'll have to come with me." She turned to Helen. "And you'll have to be me."

"Why do I feel that they should be playing the funeral march in the background?" Lauren whispered to Alice as they crossed the street, heading from the parking lot to the club. Clare was ahead, walking as if this were just a regular day in court. Not that she would ever wear such a short skirt before a judge.

Alice tucked her arm into her friend's. "Don't worry about it. This isn't a showdown. It should be fun."

The line went all the way around the block. With her usual bravado, Clare ignored everyone and headed straight to the door where the bouncer was giving favors to ladies of the hour. The three other women followed, knowing that this was one place where seniority was not measured by age.

"Back of the line!" a man, too drunk to hold himself straight, screamed at them. He tottered dangerously and would have fallen if his friends hadn't propped him up. "He said *ladies*. Not crones."

"We're neither." Clare glared at him. She was almost half his size—if that much. But he could barely stand on his two feet, and she did have all that courtroom experience. So when she pulled herself up and stared him down, Lauren almost believed her friend was a giant among women. And when Clare spoke, any remaining doubt left.

"We're secret agents on a special mission investigating how minors try to get into clubs." Clare crossed her arms and gave him the once-over. "Did I say minors? Sorry. I meant morons."

"Did she jwest call me a m-moron?" the brute slurred. She ignored him and addressed one of the bouncers.

"Excuse me, we'd like to…"

Lauren didn't hear the rest of the negotiations because someone was tugging on the expensive jacket she had borrowed from Clare for the occasion. She looked up to see the other bouncer addressing her.

"Hello, Mrs. Gard," he said. A smile transformed his bulldog features, which normally would have terrorized the angriest of crowds and the meanest of drunks, into an angelic expression.

"Why, Tad!" Lauren said with a big smile. "It is Tad? Jeff's Tad? Why, this is a surprise! I haven't seen you since your high school graduation."

Judging by his condition that night, he probably didn't remember. He'd been so happy he'd finally finished high school, he had celebrated a bit too exuberantly. Lauren had had to drive him home that night while Jeff, who had drunk almost as much, held a paper bag to his mouth.

"Yeah, it's been a while. How's Jeff? I don't hear from him much now that he's moved west. Is he around tonight, too?" Tad looked around, as if searching for her son, then turned back to Lauren, a questioning look on his face. "I didn't think he liked this kind of music."

"No, he's not here tonight. But I'll tell him I saw you. He'll be glad to have some news, I'm sure."

"It's, um, kinda funny to see you here. Not your scene, either, I wudda thought."

Lauren shrugged. "Yeah, well, um, I, am, well, here because, um, she's here." Lauren, suddenly remembering who she was not, pointed at Helen. "She works for the *Chicago Gazette* and has an invitation."

A puzzled look crossed Tad's face. "So why didn't she come with a guy? Or some girls? We're always short on girls, here."

Lauren opened her mouth to ask Tad what he thought she was, but Clare yanked her arm to indicate they were entering the club. Lauren waved goodbye and followed.

"Have a good evening, Mrs. Gard. Say hi to Jeff for me," Tad called out after her, making her feel more like a mother than she wanted.

The place was crowded, smoke-filled and noisy. Clare hustled the three of them across the floor to one of the few tables with stools.

"We must be the only females here whose belly buttons aren't showing," Lauren said, scanning the room closely to make sure there were no other hidden surprises. Meeting one of her children's friends was more than enough. If another one showed up, she wanted to be ready to duck.

"That's because our bellies are so big," Alice said. "You'd have to spend a week looking for the piercing."

"Speak for yourself. My belly is nice and flat," Clare protested. Alice raised her eyebrows, and Clare conceded. "Well, okay, maybe it's just nice."

"Helen's must be both nice and flat. Why isn't she showing hers?"

"She's trying to make sure we fit in," Alice said, shouting louder now that the band had begun to warm up. "Speaking of which, I think we should try a bit harder ourselves. Anyone up for it?"

"I suppose I should try, but I just don't see how it's done. No wonder young people complain about not being able to meet that special someone. How can they even carry on a conversation?"

"Sweetheart, I don't think it's a conversation they're after. Come on, let's go closer to the stage." Alice slid off her stool and held out a hand.

But Lauren declined. She worked on her beer while Clare, Helen and Alice moved over the crowded floor and closer to the stage. Every now and then, Lauren caught a glimpse of them, waving their arms, shaking their hips or jumping up and down. Helen was getting more than her share of admiring glances, which really didn't surprise Lauren. Funny what the right clothes and a little change of attitude could do. She would bet anything that Helen could have her choice of boyfriend now, if she only realized it. Losing her single status shouldn't be a problem for the column, as long as she was discrete.

Helen would be all right, Lauren reassured herself and focused on Alice. She had forgotten what a good dancer she was, better than many of the twenty-some-things on the floor. At least she had a sense of rhythm, something which these kids, nurtured on the steady bass beat of disco and techno, didn't.

Lauren was obviously not the only one who thought so. A man closer to Helen's age than to Alice's moved in on Alice and began dancing in step with her. It took a moment before she caught on, then the two of them broke into a clever routine. Nothing fancy, of course. It wasn't that kind of music, and Alice was not in that kind of shape. But it was enough to clear some space around them. When the song was over, everyone clapped as much for them as for the band.

With that success, Alice wasn't ready to stop. Neither were Clare or Helen. Lauren didn't understand how they managed. All she wanted to do was throw away the painful shoes she was wearing. She would also like to go home, take a bath, get into her flannel pajamas and read a book. Instead she lifted the beer to her lips.

"Ouch!" she screamed at a sudden jabbing pain in her back. Shocked, she turned around to see what had caused it.

"Sorry about that," a twenty-something man behind her said. He leaned closer to make sure she could hear him. "Are you okay?"

"I'm fine. Really."

She wasn't, but if she said so he'd probably call the cardio-mobile and send her straight to the geriatric ward. Besides, he hadn't done it intentionally. Considering the size of the crowd, it was amazing it hadn't happened before.

"Don't worry about it."

He nodded and continued to elbow his way across the floor.

Lauren stared at the half-empty glass of beer in her hand. So now, in addition to her aching feet, throbbing head and tear-filled eyes, she had a lingering pain in her back. Not to mention a very wet shirt that made her smell like a drunk.

But smell was one thing she didn't have to worry about until she left this place. It blended in nicely with the general reek of body odor and cheap perfume, alcohol and smoke.

Lauren pushed off her stool and carefully put her two feet on the ground.

"Excuse me," she said and shoved her way toward the restroom. "Excuse me. Coming through. Coming through."

There was a long line at the ladies' room, and no line outside the men's. Some things never change. It had been the same the last time she had gone clubbing, way back when, in the B.C. era—the Before Chrissie era.

Lauren took her place and waited, eavesdropping on the conversations, in search of material for her column. One woman was giving a lively account of the three exes she had run into tonight—two of whom were now dating. Another woman was hoping she would get to the bathroom before her date found her. Apparently, he wasn't what she had expected and she wanted to go home without him.

"I think I'm going to be sick," the woman behind Lauren said.

She threw up on Lauren's feet.

Clare left Alice and Helen on the dance floor. Her body was bruised from all the pushing and shoving, her ears completely shot from the screaming fans and ever-intoning bass. She was sweating more than she did in the humid Chicago summers. She needed some air. More than that, she needed fluids.

She headed for the bar, elbowing her way when necessary, dodging the drunks and the half-drunks if she could. She didn't want any alcohol stains on her blouse.

She leaned against the bar and tried to catch the barman's eye. Apparently, she wasn't showing enough cleavage, because he served a more scantily dressed blonde first. Clare clicked her tongue, knowing it wouldn't make a difference.

"Clare, I didn't know you were a fan."

"Oh hello, Anton. I could say the same about you."

Anton Muller had somehow materialized in front of her. He had traded in his conservative lawyer-wear for jeans and a tight-fitting T-shirt that revealed just how much he had been working out lately. His curly salt-and-pepper hair looked as if it had been finger-combed, contributing to a rugged look she associated more with his former profession as a cop—although if he walked his beat in that outfit, he probably could have caused a riot.

Good thing she had come with the girls or she might have forgotten her promise to herself and jumped him.

Whatever would the office gossips say then?

"I'm not really a fan," she said, brushing her hair off her face, discretely wiping away some moisture. She probably looked like a river rat. "I hadn't heard of this group until a week ago. But the music is nice. For dancing, I mean. Are you?"

"Oh, I stopped making a fool of myself long ago. Now I just watch other people do it. Not that anyone here is as foolish-looking as I was."

Clare couldn't imagine him looking foolish. "Actually, I meant are you a fan?"

"Not of this group, but I do like to check out the music scene every now and then. I know the…"

The drummer chose that moment to demonstrate his talents. With the volume up so high, Clare didn't hear the rest of Anton's words. She pointed to her ears and raised her shoulders. He smiled and shrugged.

They stood there for a minute or so, and then he jerked his head toward the bar. She tried not to look at the throat and neck muscles exposed by his slow movement.

"Can I get you something? The way I remember it, I owe you one."

"I thought we had agreed to forget about that," she practically screamed. "But thank you. I'd like some water, please."

"Just water? Not something a bit stronger?"

"Not tonight. My turn to drive."

She didn't want to tell him she hadn't touched anything stronger since that other night. It had been too close a call for her, too close to the slippery slope that had taken her father.

Anton ordered a beer and some mineral water, instantly commanding the barman's attention. Funny how Clare could win some of the biggest divorce settlements in the Windy City, outtalk the most smarmy, court-smart lawyers, but when it came to a bar, a man and a half-naked blonde won hands down.

For some reason, she didn't feel too annoyed. It was nice to let someone else do the fighting for a change. It had been such a long time since someone had taken care of her.

"You're with someone? The guy from the other night?"

"The guy who…? Oh God, no! I haven't seen him again, not since he stood me up. Tonight, I'm out with the girls." She set her glass on the counter. "Speaking of which, I'd better get back to them, or they'll think I've passed out or something. Thanks for the water, Anton."

She turned to go, wanting as much distance between them as possible. The water hadn't refreshed her. She was still feeling as hot and bothered as when she had left the floor. More maybe. Because running into Anton hadn't helped.

Clare headed toward the exit sign. The cool night

air greeted her as she stepped out into the concrete courtyard. She leaned against the wall, inhaling slowly and deeply, purging her lungs, cleaning her mind. She could still hear the drums roll and the guitars twang, but beyond that came the sounds of the city—a car screeching to a sudden stop, a siren screaming in the distance, the El clanging on its way to the next station.

"I thought you might want some more," a familiar voice said. Embarrassed, Clare turned around. Anton had obviously noticed she hadn't joined her friends.

It wasn't a glass of water she wanted so desperately, but she took it from him anyway, careful that their hands didn't touch. He seemed to notice her hesitation because he made no move to come closer. But he didn't leave, either. "You seem very tense," he said. "A night out with friends usually has the opposite effect. Is something wrong, Clare?"

"Nothing's wrong. I find it hard to tune out sometimes."

"I'd offer to help you there, but something tells me you won't appreciate it."

He took two steps forward, so that only an inch separated them. She would have had to tilt her head way back to see his face, but she was very happy looking at the broad expanse of his chest, his full shoulders, his muscled arms in that body-clinging T-shirt.

"So what do you say? Want to see how good I am?"

What the hell? You only live once. And maybe after

Anton, she would be ready to die. "Give it your best shot," she said.

He took the glass from her hand and placed it on the ground away from them. She watched as he returned to her. He reached for her shoulders, but he didn't pull her closer for a kiss. Instead, he swung her around, so that her back was facing him. Unsure of what he was up to, uncertain she could trust him, she wanted to turn back, but his strength bore down on her, not allowing her to look anywhere but forward.

"Drop your arms," he said. "Just let them go. Imagine they're a weight you've been carrying. Release your hold, and let go."

She couldn't have lifted her arms if she tried. They were limp and light.

"It's a simple relaxation technique I picked up a long time ago," he said.

"When you were a cop?" she asked, realizing she might be crossing some invisible lines. They never talked about their personal lives.

"Yes." He paused and then continued. "There's a lot of stress when you're a cop, and not a lot of ways to deal with it. But this technique works. You can try it anywhere really. Do it again. Good," he said. "Now try the same thing with your head. Bend it forward slowly, feel the muscles stretch? Can you feel that tension in your neck? Okay, now, let go."

Her head was floating like a buoy on water.

"Okay. Now we're really ready to begin."

His fingers gently stroked her nape, his touch light. Then he slowly increased pressure, broadening his strokes, using his thumb, then his knuckles. He began to knead her shoulders, relieving her tension, unburdening her. She felt so relaxed, so liberated she didn't notice him stopping, didn't realize it was no longer his hands against her nape, but his breath, not until he brushed his lips against the base of her neck and kissed her.

One small kiss. One nuclear-power reaction.

It sent quivers through her whole body. She thought her feet would give way and that she was going to melt into a mass on the floor. But, no, she was still standing.

"I think we should stop there," he said, his voice unusually thick.

She didn't turn to face him. "It would be better."

"Unless you want to go some place else." His voice was almost a whisper. "Then we could try something else."

After the way he had touched her, her whole body was saying, singing, screaming, "Yes! Yes! Yes!" She wanted to try all kinds of things with him. Wanted to spend all night trying.

But then what? Where would they be when it came to working their cases together? Where would they be when it came to attributing the Van Belden account? And if anyone found out...

She shook her head, not trusting herself to speak.

After a moment, she turned and looked him in the eye. She owed him that much.

"No. I think that's enough for tonight. Not that I didn't appreciate it. It was wonderful. Just what I needed. I'm a new woman, who needs to go find her friends. So if you'll just let me…"

He wouldn't move out of her way, so she stepped around him, toward the door.

"Clare?"

She looked back.

"Is it me? Because I would swear there's something between us. Because we…" He moved his hands in the space between them, pointing at the two of them. "I mean, we are, we could…" He dropped his hands. "You know."

"Of course, there's nothing wrong with you, Anton. But we work together. I have a rule against it. I know from experience, that it really isn't a good idea." She looked up at the glowing night sky and then back at him. "And even if I weren't against the idea in principle, there is the Van Belden account."

"The Van Belden account? What does that—"

"I will be deciding who gets it. Just today I was looking at your file and several others. I wouldn't want to be accused of favoritism."

And I'm sure you wouldn't want to be accused of sleeping your way to the top, she wanted to say. But she didn't. She didn't want him to think the idea had even crossed her mind. She didn't want to explain why it might.

He shrugged. "If that's how you feel."

"It's for the best."

"So, I guess I'll see you around then."

"Yes, see you on Monday." She paused briefly at the door. "And, Anton, thanks for the massage. It really helped."

She walked through the door and right into Lauren.

CHAPTER 9

"I can still smell vomit on me. I mean, I know I've dealt with it loads of times with my own kids, but, really, if ever there was a sign that I shouldn't be writing this column, that was it."

Lauren put down her teacup. After the evening had turned from fiasco to all-out catastrophe, she had decided to leave. Her friends had insisted on going with her, even though Alice and Helen were still going strong on the dance floor. Feeling guilty for ending their night so soon, Lauren had invited them to her house for tamer entertainment. How much tamer could you get than late-night tea and conversation?

Helen hadn't even been up for that. She had gone to her room after one cup of tea, leaving the older women to discuss the events of the evening.

"Oh, I don't know about that," Alice said. "You were wondering how singles connect in noisy clubs. You just discovered a new meaning for 'pick up.'"

"As in, 'I'll pick up your mess after you,'" Clare said.

Lauren didn't laugh. She looked from Alice to Clare. "What was I supposed to do?"

"The same thing any sensible thirty-year-old would do. Wipe your shoes, then speak to the sick culprit long enough to get an address to send the bill for a new pair of shoes," Clare said in her best lawyer voice.

Alice agreed. "You didn't have to wipe her face with a cold cloth."

"Or get her water."

"Or hold her hand."

"I couldn't just leave her," Lauren said in her own defense. "I could have been her mother."

"That's probably why she didn't keep throwing up. She was so terrified you *were* her mother!"

"My point exactly!" Lauren threw her hands up in the air. "How can I write about the experiences of a twenty- or thirty-year-old, when everyone takes me for their fifty-year-old mother? Which is only half as bad as actually *being* their mother."

"It's in your head, Lauren." Alice exhaled, as if expelling her impatience. "Nobody thought I was anybody's mother. That guy I danced with, he was probably learning how to walk the same time my kids were, but that didn't stop him. We danced well together. I know he thought so because he asked me if I was a regular."

"Really?!"

"Yes. Really. He said we should try it out some more."

"What did you say?"

"Only if my kids didn't ground me for staying out too late." She grinned. "Seriously? I said we'll see."

"Because you'd actually go back there again?"

"I might. It made me realize how much I liked dancing. I wouldn't mind doing it some more. And it is great exercise for these menopausal bones, and a heck of a lot more fun than some of those fitness classes I've taken."

"So why don't you go with Frank? I thought he liked dancing," Lauren said.

"Not as much as he likes watching the idiot box. I asked him if he wanted to come tonight. He said MTV's *Rockers Unplugged Special* was on, and he didn't want to miss it. *Rockers Unplugged!*" Alice rolled her eyes. "If anyone needs unplugging, it's him!"

Lauren didn't like what she was hearing, especially when Alice had confessed recently that her marriage was becoming more of a chore than anything else. Lauren hadn't realized that encouraging Alice to pull Frank away from the television would mean that her friend would end up pulling herself away and going solo.

"So you would seriously get together with some stranger because you like dancing? You would ruin a twenty-five-year-old marriage for that?"

"Whoa!" Alice lifted her hands in the air. "Slow down, Lauren. How did we go from dancing to ruining a marriage?"

Lauren bit down on her tongue.

"Look, all I'm saying is I'm done with the stay-at-home

routine he wants," Alice continued. "If he won't come out with me, I'll have to go on my own. Or with you."

Lauren opened her mouth, but Alice held up a finger.

"So you better have more outings lined up for us. You can't quit just because this one ended badly."

Clare nodded in agreement. "She's right, Lauren. And it wasn't that much of a disaster."

"Not for me. That's for sure," Alice said. "Besides, Lauren, you could turn all of this to your advantage. I mean it doesn't have to be about all the horrible stuff that happened to *you*. It could be about how great it was for *me*."

"Or the girl who vomited. Think where she would be if you weren't there. With her head propped up against a toilet bowl." Clare moved her head in a poor attempt to show what it might have looked like.

Alice laughed. "Silly Clare. I don't think her tongue would be sticking out quite like that."

Clare brought her head back up. "Probably not. Anyway, if everything worked out fine, there would be nothing to write about. You need failures. They're part of the learning experience, yours and the readers'. You're the writer, Lauren. You should know that."

"If it's worth anything," Alice said. "I'm glad I came. I would probably be home watching *Rockers Unplugged*. Or last year's NBA championships, which never makes any sense to me."

"Me, too. I'd be at home working on another case."

"Instead of working on another man?" Lauren said, watching Clare closely.

"I wasn't working *on* another man." A red flush crept up her face. It couldn't have been the alcohol because as the designated driver Clare hadn't touched the stuff. "I work *with* him."

"Uh-huh. I was there, Clare. Remember? I saw you."

Actually, Lauren had arrived too late to see much more than Clare coming in from the courtyard, an athletic-looking man on her heels. She'd been flustered and embarrassed, as if she had been caught at some illicit assignation that hadn't gone well, not if the mixture of frustration and tenderness and embarrassment on both their faces was anything to go by.

"It can't go anywhere." Clare ran her manicured fingers through her drooping curls. "Like I said, we work together."

"So? Happens all the time," Alice said. "There's a married couple who work in the same division at my bank. They don't seem to have any problems."

"It's not the same thing. He doesn't just work *with* me. He works *for* me. In fact, his future in the firm depends *on* me." Clare laughed nervously. "He's one of several associates we're looking at to handle a major account."

"And you think—"

"That he might be coming on to me because of that? It's a possibility."

Lauren shook her head vigorously. "I don't believe it. I saw how he was looking at you."

Clare shrugged. "It won't be the first time a man tried to sleep his way to the top—and enjoyed it."

"I thought only women did that."

"Are you kidding? Believe me. I know. It's happened."

"To you?"

"Yes, actually, to me."

Alice reached out to squeeze her hand. "Oh, Clare."

Clare pulled her hand away. "It doesn't matter. It was a long time ago. I was very young." She laughed without humor. "And very naive, very, very naive."

"But it's not the same guy," Lauren said. "Don't you want to give this one a chance?"

"Not really. We're much better off remaining colleagues."

But from the way Clare avoided her eyes, Lauren suspected she wasn't telling the truth.

Helen looked up from the computer printouts she was examining and smiled at Joe Bardet, seated opposite her at a coffee shop. "You might want to think about using a database for that. There's an *xtml* coding that could be useful here, too. And the c-imaging here…" Helen stopped, realizing she had said too much.

What did Lauren Wilt the writer know about computer programming and Web designing? And why would she be giving hints to a pro? If Joe had called her to discuss the Web site—which Lauren had finally agreed to do—then he was a pro who had a job to get done.

And come to think of it, so did she. She was on an impossible mission where failure was not an alternative. Not for Lauren. Not for her. All the more reason to remember that guys like Joe didn't flirt with Helen the Geek. Guys like Joe didn't like smart women. So why was she doing everything to blow her cover?

Helen looked up cautiously and eyed Joe over her coffee cup. His face was inscrutable. At least Helen had always thought that's what an inscrutable face would look like. She didn't often come across such faces, even though they were abundant in the novels she read.

"You know something about programming?" Joe asked.

"A little. I took some classes a while ago."

Which was the truth, nothing but the truth, so help her, God. God wouldn't mind if there was a little less of it than usual, would he? Was understatement even mentioned in the small print of the Ten Commandments?

"Yeah?" Joe said. "That's funny. So did I. I kind of figured being an English major wouldn't pay for my apartment. It doesn't even pay for my breakfast bagel. So here I am, working on Web designing instead. But as you've probably figured, I suck at it. You'd probably be much better. Wanna trade jobs?"

He wriggled his eyebrows. Helen did her best Valley Girl high-pitched giggle imitation and shook her head. If only he knew.

"Just kidding," he said.

"You don't suck at it," Helen reassured him, giving the layout he had brought to show her a second glance. "Sometimes two heads are better than one. The other person picks up things you don't see. Like, you know, an editor or a proofreader."

"Maybe you're right. I don't show my drafts to the others because I... I don't want them to know how bad I am at it. I couldn't believe it when they gave me the job. I was just about to apply for a job at the local MacDonald's."

He sounded so glum, she almost believed him. "Really?"

"No." He made a funny sound. "But it was pretty bad. I'm thinking of going to grad school eventually, but I thought I'd try my hand in the real world first. It's pretty cruel out there. Out here, I mean."

"But you got this job."

"Sure. And I'll probably blow it."

"You know, if you want to show your work to someone, you can, um, show it to me."

She winced internally. Why had she said that? Why had she offered? Helen the Geek was back. She needed to get rid of her fast. Where are you, Lauren the Swinging Single Chick, when we need you?

"It *is* about, um, my column." Then, without even thinking twice, she tilted her head and looked at Joe from under her eyelashes. "Not that I know very much more."

"No, that's good," Joe said with a smile. "That's very good. You're right. Two heads are better than one."

They sat there with the layout between them, grinning at each other. Well, she hoped she looked like she was grinning. All she knew was that her mouth couldn't move and her heart had stopped, and no one had ever smiled at her like that. Of course, Joe wasn't really smiling at her. He was smiling at Lauren. But at this point, Helen would accept anything she could get.

Joe cleared his throat. "I read your column last week."

"Oh?"

"Yeah. It wasn't what I was expecting."

"No?"

"It's different."

"Different?" She paused for a minute, then nodded. "Oh, you mean it's different from the things you normally read? *Dr. Dobb's Journal, Programmer's Manual, PC World*, that kind of thing?"

Which were the kinds of things she read, the things programmers read.

He gave her a funny look and said, "I guess you read around a lot. I mean, sure, I read that stuff. I have to, to keep up, you know. But I read a lot of women's magazines, too. I have two older sisters, and they never learned what 'tidy up' means. They left their stuff all over the place. Including *Seventeen* and *Cosmo*. I learned more about women reading that than watching the adult channels." He coughed loudly. "Oops. I didn't mean what that sounds like. Really. I don't want you thinking that."

"I understand."

But she didn't. Then, she thought of her own brothers and what channels they watched and what channels they wouldn't let her watch. Oh no! Not Joe! She felt a sudden flash of heat attack her cheeks.

He must have noticed because he was shaking his head very firmly. "Really, I didn't, not a lot of it, not more than other guys." He looked up at the ceiling, then across the floor, then finally back at her. He cleared his throat. "So, anyway, as I was saying, your column's different from most of that stuff. You don't whine as much. You're not out to reform men. You preach being yourself. I like that."

"Kind of you to say so." Helen fluttered her eyes at him à la Carrie Bradshaw.

"No, I mean it. I like your writing. But there's something about it, I don't get. It doesn't sound exactly like you. At least, what I've seen of you."

"Now that's funny, since I put my heart and soul in it."

What's a little white lie for a good friend? Were *those* mentioned in the Ten Commandments?

"The shoes, for one," he said, moving slightly so he had her silver-strapped sandals in full view. "Those aren't exactly what came to mind when I read your piece about 'sole mates.'"

Helen didn't have the slightest idea what he was

talking about. She really should read Lauren's column more closely if she wanted to continue to impersonate her.

"Oh, that!" she said. "The other pair didn't quite, um, match with this skirt. Besides, I am not what I write. Isn't that the first rule of fiction?"

"But this isn't fiction."

"It is, kind of. I've got a point to get across. Sometimes I exaggerate a bit. I think that's okay."

"I'm not so sure. What about your ethics as a journalist? Isn't it your duty to report the truth and nothing but the truth? Haven't there been enough scandals lately, giving newspapers a bad name? You don't want to add to that, do you?"

His pace quickened as he spoke, his cheeks grew brighter. This obviously meant a lot to him. Helen was genuinely surprised. She had thought he was just another beautiful coverboy, but he was much more than that. He had convictions and beliefs that she would agree with in any other circumstances.

She shook her head vigorously. "I don't think I'm being unethical."

"But you're not telling the whole truth."

"But I'm not reporting, either. I'm observing, commenting, speculating. There's a lot more room for half-truths in what I'm doing than in most journalistic genres." She blew air into her bangs as she struggled to defend herself. If he was ticked off about this, what would he say when he knew the truth?

"It's not as if I'm reporting on international news or political scandals. In those instances, you really do have to tell the truth."

That seemed to convince him because he nodded. "Okay, you win, the same rules don't apply. Which leaves me with a problem," he said, his eyes fixed on her face.

"How am I going to find out about you? The *real* you, I mean."

Did that mean... Oh God! Was he *flirting* with her? No. He couldn't be. Then why? She was trying so hard to work it out that she almost missed the rest of his questions.

"...have to do to know? Invite you out for a drink or something?"

"Like on a date?" Helen hoped he didn't hear the sound she made in her throat as she gulped. A date! With him! A real date with a man, who wasn't a bore. Okay, he was a computer programmer, but not a very good one, not a very dedicated one. She could go on a date with him.

No, she couldn't.

"I, um, don't think it would be a very good idea. I would have to write about it, you know. You might not like that."

"I would be on my best behavior. So there wouldn't be anything bad to say."

He smiled, and Helen almost said yes. When? Right now? Let's go. But she didn't. She shook her head and let Lauren speak. "We work together. I don't think it's a good idea to mix, um, you know, business and, um, you know, pleasure."

"So that would be a no?"

"No. Yes." She set her flapping hands on the table, weaving one into the other to keep them down. "I mean, yes, that would be a no. But maybe you could, um, ask me again after six months. Or, um, maybe I could ask you. Since you read *Cosmo* and *Vogue* and have sisters and stuff."

"Yeah, you could ask me."

"After this is over," she insisted, making sure he understood.

"After this is over. It's a deal."

He held out his hand to close their agreement. She hesitated about giving him hers. It was one thing to exaggerate and to lie. It was something else to give her hand and her word. But she wouldn't break their bargain. When this was over, she would ask him out. Only she was pretty certain he wouldn't want to know the real her then, not once he knew the truth.

Helen put her hand in Joe's. It wasn't the feel of his big, strong, masculine clasp that practically short-circuited her internal wiring. It was something that reached to her from behind the dark depths of his eyes, something she recognized, something she thought only happened in books.

They sat like that for a moment, their hands clasped, their eyes meeting. When she finally began to think clearly, she wondered whether some magic spell had turned them to stone. It took an immeasurable effort to withdraw her hand. It dropped into her lap.

"Now, about that Web site…" Helen said, trying to sound less like a romance heroine and more like a professional journalist. She did have to report back to Lauren, after all. But maybe not about the new prospects in her love life—that, she would keep for Chrissie.

"Here's someone who wants to know where you learned to be so funny," Helen told Lauren, helping to sort through the letters she'd brought back from her latest meeting at the *Chicago Gazette*.

"Put it in the To Be Answered pile, for now. Keep track of it, though. If there are more like that, we can put them with the Frequently Asked Questions." Lauren swiveled her chair around and continued to read her letters.

"I need to know what 'my' readers think," Helen said. "Now that I am the official face of Lauren Wilt."

Lauren thought Helen was taking the favor a bit too seriously, and although she wasn't sure they had the same ideas about organization, she was grateful for the help. She didn't want Sherelle or her editorial assistant in the way, not with the secret she had to hide.

So she was letting Helen into her sanctuary, a sanctuary that no one else had dared to enter, not her children or her husband.

So far she didn't regret it. On the contrary, Lauren was surprised at how much she enjoyed Helen's insights and company. Helen was fun to be with. And if her messiness continued to be irritating, Lauren also found it endearing, just as she did Chrissie's stubbornness, Jeff's dedication, Clare's cynicism and Alice's optimism. Accepting flaws was a part of every close relationship, and Helen had become her friend.

"What about this one?" Helen said now, her eyes on one of the letters. "It looks like a marriage proposal."

Lauren swiveled around. "You're joking?!"

"*I'm* not, but maybe he is. Here's what he says— 'Lauren, you are the one I have *always* been waiting for. Your words are like pearls of wisdom I hold dearer than my heart. Please say "yes" and put me out of my misery.'"

"Sounds like he needs a lot more than 'yes' to be put out of his misery. Sounds like he needs a hole in his head. Correction. He already has a hole in his head. He needs it filled in."

"You don't think it's sweet?"

Lauren looked over the top of her glasses. Nothing in Helen's expression said she wasn't serious.

"For a kid who was brought up by her father and two brothers, you're a very romantic person. For a computer whiz, you're a very romantic person. For a woman of today, you're a very romantic person." Lauren shook her head in mock dismay, waved her hand and continued.

"I'm sorry to have to break it to you, Helen, but you should thank your lucky stars you haven't met anyone who says things like that. And if you do, don't believe him. Just don't."

Lauren wanted to continue with the lecture, but decided to spare Helen. She had been young and naive once, too. She had been a believer, and no one could have talked her out of it. She doubted she could convince Helen otherwise, not that she didn't wish she could.

Lauren waited for the familiar tightening of her chest and the drying of her throat, the reaction that came whenever she thought of her failed marriage and how, in one year, her life had all come tumbling down. Nothing happened. She blinked her eyes to chase back the tears. There weren't any.

Lauren smiled with relief at a wide-eyed Helen holding up the letter.

"So where *does* it go? The trash?" Helen asked.

"No, don't throw it away. You never know, I may want to do something on the dark side of romantic love. Do we have a file for psychos?"

"For psychos? You don't mean…" The surprised look on Helen's face was priceless. "Oh my God, Lauren! What if he's serious and he can't forget you? What if he starts to follow you? Like a stalker or something? Oh my God!" Helen's expression changed to real horror. "But he wouldn't go after you. He would go after me. I'm the official face of Lauren. It would be just like that movie where—"

"It's not like that movie, and he's not going to go after anyone," Lauren assured her. "If he does, we'll do what Sherelle said and send him to her."

Helen's openmouthed look of fear did not go away. Lauren took the letter from her and shoved it into one of her piles. "Seriously, Helen, don't worry about it. It's just a joke. We're public people now. We're attracting lots of attention. If we weren't we should be worried." When Helen's face still didn't change, Lauren continued. "I've seen weirder than this. You wouldn't believe some of the things I got after *Autobiography of a House* came out. Tell me what you make of this one."

Determined to change the subject, Lauren read one of the letters she had been examining. "'My parents think I should go to law school, but lawyers just aren't my type. I want more adventure in my life. I've always dreamed of sailing around the world. Do you think I should settle?'"

She put the letter down. "So, official face of Lauren, what would you say?"

"I think she should do what she wants to do. Parents don't always know what's best."

Lauren wondered if that came from personal experience. She didn't know much about Helen and her family, except that she'd been brought up by her dad and two brothers. She'd have to ask Chrissie. "Well, since I'm a parent, I *should* say law school. But then, some potential lawyer she is, if she thinks 'settling' is about staying in one place or that law school is some kind of marriage market."

Lauren leaned back in her swivel chair. "You know, I never thought I'd get this much mail."

"But you said people wrote to you before, after your book was published. Chrissie said it was a big success. You were interviewed and—"

Lauren waved her hand to stop Helen. "Sure some readers wrote to me."

"So it's not so surprising?"

"Not that part of it." Lauren looked at the piles of letters. "You're right. People like to share their reactions and experiences, but the thing that surprises me about these letters is that the people writing them are asking for advice. But this is a singles column, not an advice sheet."

"But don't you want to give them advice?"

Lauren sighed. "I thought I was doing that by writing the column, but they want more, and I'm not sure I can give it. When people wrote to me about my book, I sent out a form letter. Sometimes, when I was moved, I would add a little note. But that dealt with a different subject. Now, I don't know." She rolled up to the table and rested her head on her arms. "I guess that's what the Web site is supposed to do."

"Not everyone is asking for advice. Here's a very nice letter. 'Dear Lauren,'" Helen read. "'Your description of girl's night at the club really struck a chord. I used to go to clubs to meet men. Now I just go to listen to the music. I really enjoy myself and I don't feel so let down when I go home alone. You are so right when you say we singles should live for the present rather than for our lives down the road.'" Helen put the letter down. "She's not asking for anything. She's just saying thank-you."

Lauren smiled, feeling a comforting warmth spreading through her. Maybe it didn't matter that she and Helen were carrying on a deception if they could touch someone like that.

But it wasn't so simple.

"Not everyone likes me." She shuffled through a pile until she found what she was looking for. "Listen, 'Single stands for selfish and self-centered. You don't understand that it takes two to make a couple. No wonder you are still alone.'"

"What an awful thing to say!" Helen said. "Whoever wrote that really doesn't know what she's saying!"

"Oh, I don't know. She's not entirely wrong. I *am* writing this column for completely selfish reasons. All I care about is my house. Keeping it, I mean."

"Still. You *are* making a difference, Lauren. And besides, like that other letter said, it's not why *you* are doing it, it's what the reader gets out of it." Helen crossed her arms and stuck out her chin. "I think you should answer that letter. I think you should tell that person she's wrong about you, about singles, about us."

Lauren contemplated Helen for a moment. She'd never imagined the girl could have such conviction.

"Maybe you're right," she said. "Maybe I will answer that letter. Maybe I just will."

CHAPTER 10

Single stands for selfish and self-centered.

Lauren read the sentence once again. Selfish and self-centered? Because we're looking out for ourselves? Because we're choosy? Is that a bad thing? What's wrong with holding out for the best? What's wrong with believing in a Mr. Right?

She had done that once.

She could still remember meeting Charles at Northwestern when they had both been sophomores. She had arrived late for the casting of some now-forgotten pretentious play with an existential message. He had already taken his position and was in the midst of reciting the lines of the angst-ridden hero. Like everyone else, she fell under his spell.

It seemed too good to be true when she realized he was falling for her, too. At first, she chalked it up to a stage effect: She had been cast as one of the more important secondary characters, and she and Charles were thrown together. But soon they were spending more time together off stage than on it, which continued even after the short run of their amateurish production. When he left at the end of the year to attend a prestigious business school in Boston, they pursued their long-distance relationship with more regularity than many couples who lived on the same campus.

So, the following year when Lauren graduated, it made sense for her to look for a job in the Boston area. It made even more sense for Charles to propose two years later, and that she should accept. Because despite being thoroughly modern, a card-carrying member of The National Organization of Women and a supporter of equal rights for women, Lauren clung to the very traditional dream of happily ever after. While her college friends were pursuing careers with fervor, Lauren opted to be a stay-at-home wife, choosing to be an appendage to her husband and her children.

Well, not exactly an appendage.

When Charles was offered a lucrative position at the Chicago headquarters of a multinational conglomerate, she was delighted to return to her roots, insisting on moving into the crumbling Victorian she had recently inherited from her suffragist grandmother. It was Charles's one concession—he would have preferred something more extravagant, more grandiose, more fitting with the position he occupied. But drawn by childhood memories, she put her foot down. They settled into their Oak Park residence, and she made a career out of renovating and restoring the house.

For a while, it had seemed as if she had it all: husband, house, children, career. Then, her world had collapsed faster than an undercooked soufflé.

Was she wrong to have believed in it? Was she wrong to have wanted it? To want it again? Of course not, no more than all the other hopeful singles she wrote to and for. And if those dreams and ambitions made her selfish and self-centered, she'd wear those labels like badges of honor.

It takes two to make a couple? Wrong. Sometimes it just takes one.

For years, Lauren had bolstered her marriage. Her singular efforts had begun as early as her move to Boston and continued until the children left for college. She had been understanding when Charles didn't make it to dinner, forgiving when he worked through holidays, accepting when he missed the children's parties and performances.

Two to make a couple? Charles just hadn't been there. He had been in his office, working his way up the corporate ladder, or perhaps, more likely, working his way down some woman's blouse.

She discovered Charles's first infidelity a year after Jeff was born. Or maybe he was two, because he was already stringing words together. "No cry, no cry," he'd said when she was unable to stop the tears running down her cheeks. Charles's secretary had confirmed that he wasn't in his office. He was with another woman in a downtown hotel, where he had been spotted by one of Lauren's mother's gossipy acquaintances.

Lauren turned to pick up Jeff and caught a glimpse of herself in the bedroom mirror. She was wearing an oversized sweatshirt—probably one of Charles's, her own didn't fit anymore. Decorated with so much baby food, it looked like a Jackson Pollock painting. But that was just the icing on a very ugly cake. She looked fat from all the weight she had put on during her pregnancy with Jeff, haggard from lack of sleep, strung out from her son's toddler antics, unkempt from having ignored her makeup and her hairbrush. A bag lady who spent her nights in the El and days in the alleys looked better.

No wonder Charles had turned to another woman, she'd thought then. She confronted him, but it didn't really matter. One look in the mirror, and he was already forgiven. By the time she was pregnant with Chrissie, the incident was forgotten.

Until the next time. Then, it wasn't her mother's friend who told Lauren, and she wasn't in a postpartum nightmare. She heard from the other woman herself, one of the junior managers at Charles's company who was being let go and wanted a little revenge—at Lauren's expense.

Charles said he regretted it. It would never happen again. Lauren believed him. She forgave and forgot again.

Until Tracie. But this last, final time, Charles didn't want forgiveness and forgetting. This time, he wanted a new life, without Lauren.

It took *two* to make a couple? The reader was wrong. Sometimes it took three, four or more. And, sometimes, it did take two: one to keep it going, the other to leave.

Lauren blinked her tears away and focused on another line in the same letter. *No wonder you are still alone.* Does the writer think she's insulting me? Is being alone a bad thing?

Lauren had thought so after Charles had left. She should have been relieved that their unhappily ever after was finally over, but instead she couldn't help wondering why he had been the one to go when she had been ready to put up with so much for so long. Was being alone the punishment for having pretended everything was fine, for ignoring their troubled coexistence for so long? That had been easy enough to do with the distraction of raising children. And then, of course, there was the house.

One of many Victorians originally built for Chicago's emerging middle class, Lauren's grandmother's house was hardly unique in the architectural landscape of Oak Park, birthplace of the Prairie School design and home to a number of Frank Lloyd Wright's projects. Yet, for her, it was unique and special, full of memories and mementoes, and certainly deserving of all the attention she lavished on it.

Lauren discussed the foundations with architects, reconfigured the wiring with electricians, assessed the pipes with plumbers. She oversaw the installation of storm windows, the replacement of shingles, the gutting of interior walls. She investigated wooden floorboards, researched ornamental designs, hunted down original stained glass patterns. At a time when many of her peers preferred prefab houses and high-rise condominiums, Lauren joined an emerging movement dedicated to the restoration of old houses and the preservation of dying neighborhoods.

On a family trip to San Francisco, she saw the Victorian homes known as Painted Ladies. Their flamboyant colors and daring designs enchanted her. She was inspired to paint her own Victorian similarly. When a neighbor objected to the bright color she chose, Lauren wrote an article for the neighborhood paper about the colorful facades of the original dwellings. Nineteenth-century, middle-class owners, such as her industrialist great-grandfather and her suffragist grandmother, were as interested in expressing individuality in an age of mass production as she was currently.

Lauren's enthusiastic piece led to more articles and eventually a book, where she explored the changes inhabitants bring to a residence from the house's own point of view. Philosophical, whimsical and well researched, it had preoccupied her to the exclusion of all else.

And why not? By that time, her children were

almost grown and already halfway out of the house. Charles was pursuing his career. He didn't seem to need or want her attention. He and Lauren had drifted apart, held together only by habit. The house had been filled with his presence, but there had been no one for her to talk to. They had both checked out of their marriage a long time ago.

She should have been relieved, but those first months after the divorce had been hell. It hadn't helped that the children were gone. It hadn't helped that her second book refused to be written. Her friends and family were moving on, while she was grinding down to a slow halt.

But things had changed over the past few weeks. She was alone, but she no longer lived in solitary confinement.

Single? Yes. Alone? Sometimes. Lonely? Certainly not.

Lauren took a minute to gather her thoughts. She flexed her fingers, positioned them over the keyboard and began to type.

A reader recently commented that we singles complain too much. We want it both ways. We want the freedom of flying solo, but we also want the soft landing with other equal-minded persons. Everything and anything, as long as it doesn't put a damper on our lifestyles. "Singles," she wrote, "are selfish."

That's one way of looking at it. The others are not much better.

My married friends have stopped inviting me to their parties. When I confronted Jane about it, she said it would upset the table arrangement. Marsie had a different answer: she has a hard time finding single men for me and doesn't want me to feel like a fifth wheel. I suppose that's better than being told she's worried about me running away with one of the husbands.

Why does single have to mean frustrated and lonely-hearted?

There is one invitation I never stop getting. The one that comes with Cousin Harry, Colleague Dick or Friend Tom very firmly attached. Once it's clear you're available, everything— from well-meaning friends to reality television, from the publishing industry to the Internet— conspires to get you out of the way. Signed, sealed and married. Or at least with the intention of doing so.

Why does single have to be a disease to be cured or a scourge to be eradicated?

A couple of years ago, I met a guy with a seven-digit income and not a physical or personal blemish in sight. Once my friends heard of him, they immediately asked for the wedding date. No one noticed he bored me. Tie the knot first, and untie the difficulties later.

Why should singles always have to settle?

To all the single-tracked folks who fit the above boxes, I have this to say.

Single may be selfish, self-centered, self-serving, but it's also single-minded—in all the determination we bring to our happy lives. Single-handed—in all the dexterity with which we maneuver through a life made for couples. Single-hearted—in the sincerity, honesty and optimism of our outlook. Single-footed—in the fancy footwork needed to keep up with our married friends.

Singles are here to stay. Learn to live with us.

CHAPTER 11

"So, are things with Frank and you any better?" Lauren asked.

"No. Not really," Alice Mirosek told her.

They had finished their group exercises at the Fitness Center and were getting ready to use the machines. Fortunately, two treadmills had just been vacated next to each other, so Alice and Lauren could have a long overdue conversation.

They had been attending the Fitness Center together for almost ten years. It wasn't so much an obsession with youth as with the desire to help their bodies adjust to the menopausal softening of bones and weakening of muscles that had motivated them to sign up for an exercise regime. Lauren had worked out religiously until her divorce, when she dropped out of almost everything in her life. She was happy to be back on the treadmill again with her friend next to her.

"And I'm not sure I understand it, although I've really been trying to the last couple of weeks," Alice was saying, her hands clutching the sidebars while her feet pattered steadily. "Trying to find a way to bring us back together, I mean. But it's as if we've come to some kind of crossroad. Frank wants to deal with home repairs, I want to go dancing. He wants a snazzy new television, I want trips to Europe and Latin America. He wants to retire from life, but I'm just raring to go."

"He's not retiring, sweetie. He's slowing down. We're all slowing down."

"Not that fast. Not so everything moves in freeze-frame motion. I mean, he's more interested in watching *Survivor* than in doing anything more than surviving himself!"

Lauren thought it best to ignore the angry outburst. "And he's really not interested in anything else?"

"Nothing I can see." Alice sighed. "I've even asked him if he wants to go out with us. I've been having so much fun doing 'single' things with you, I thought he might like them, too. I mean, you don't have to be single to feel young again, to go out every now and then, do you?"

"Of course not."

"So I asked him. And he said no. It's not like him, Lauren. It's not like him, at all. He's never been the kind of guy to let life pass him by. I'm not saying he was a mover and shaker or anything. But he did things; got out of his neighborhood, went to college, got a job, a *good* job." Alice punctuated her sentence with a strong downward kick. Her breathing didn't falter. "He was so passionate about things. He really believed in everything he did. He made other people believe, too. I think of that, and I can't believe he's going to just sit it out now and watch TV."

"Maybe he's just tired, Alice." Lauren thought of herself on the machine. They'd only been going for fifteen minutes, and she already wanted to stop. "Maybe he just wants a break."

Alice certainly didn't. She was continuing with the same determination as when they started. "He's been taking a break for four years. Since Mark began college."

"Alice—"

"Okay, maybe he needs a break. But why can't he tell me that? I mean, I might not need it myself. I might not understand it." She lifted a hand off the support bar and pushed her headband back. "But if it's what he wants, I'll go along with it. As long as we can do it together. We've done everything together, and now he wants to be on his own?"

"Maybe it's difficult for him. Maybe he doesn't think you'll understand. Maybe he feels unwanted and old, like we do. Men can't be all that different from us, can they?"

Alice snorted. "I wouldn't put it past them."

"I think it's time for you two to talk things out, open up, have a heart-to-heart."

"Lauren, I'm an accountant, not much experience at heart-to-heart there. If you want heart, you go to the social worker. *That* would be *Frank*."

"So maybe he can't manage heart-to-heart in his own life."

"Frank can. At least, he could. He convinced his daughter that shaving her head was not the way to deal with tragedy. He persuaded his son that flunking algebra was not the way to rebel."

"Okay, I get your point." Lauren paced silently for a while, until she remembered something. "But who got our two daughters, Karen *and* Chrissie, through their bulimic phase?"

"You did."

"That's funny. I always thought it was you." Lauren turned off her machine, exhaling more from frustration than fatigue. "Look, Alice, all I'm saying is maybe now Frank can't open up. Or won't. Or something."

Lauren wanted to shake her friend. She wanted to give Alice a big kick in the behind, strong enough so that it would also get to Frank. Lauren knew Alice cared deeply for her husband, and she was equally certain that Frank was devoted to his wife. Charles and she had been steadily drifting farther and farther apart, but Alice and Frank had built a life together against all the odds. They couldn't let a misunderstanding and a temporary lifestyle conflict tear them apart.

"Done here?" Alice asked.

Lauren nodded. She leaned closer to her friend. "Look, Alice, do you love Frank?"

Alice answered without hesitation. "Yes. Of course, I do."

"And is this marriage important to you?"

Again, her friend's answer was unequivocal. "Yes. Of course, it is. We've been through everything together. He's my best friend, my closest buddy. I can't imagine life without him."

"Well, then, you're going to have to confront him. No more beating around the bush. Just come out with it. It's as simple as that." She wrapped her arm through Alice's. "Now, shall we take those showers?"

"Now that you're all out of steam," Alice observed a while later in the lobby, "how ever are you going to manage on your hot date tonight?"

"It's not a *hot* date. It'll probably be as horrible as the last one. My agent has been badgering me about meeting this guy for a while now. And since Louise has been so great about getting my deadline extended for *My Mother's Garden*, I just can't say no. Besides, I'm always looking for new material for the column."

"The column, the column." Alice rolled her eyes. "I think what you're doing is great, Lauren, but don't forget about your real life. That's why you're doing this, not the other way round."

"I know. I haven't forgotten." Lauren glanced at her watch. "We'd better go, or Clare will think we're standing her up."

"Where did you say we were meeting her?"

"Douce Flagrance."

"Douce… But that's a lingerie shop."

"Yes. So?"

"Why are we going to a lingerie shop? Oh." Alice stopped in the middle of the floor. "This is about your column again. You could have warned me."

Lauren continued walking; Alice followed. "It's not for my column. Well, not entirely. It's for us."

"For us? Are you kidding?" Alice looked down at her very ample chest that had probably never been contained in anything smaller than a D cup.

"You can use some fine lingerie," Lauren told her, as they headed for the garage.

"Not the kind they have at Douce Flagrance. And I can't afford anything there, anyway. The prices are way out of my range."

Lauren waved her hand dismissively. "I'm sure we'll find something. I can always put it down as expenses."

"You wouldn't!" The look on Alice's face was priceless. Lauren had to laugh.

"No, I wouldn't. But it is research. Clare says it's just the kind of fun thing a single woman does, or should do, anyway. She's all for us splurging and buying something special for ourselves. Remember how much fun we had getting our hair done?"

"That was different. Besides, I'm not single."

"From what you've been telling me, you are single with husband. Which is almost the same thing. Besides, you might need something like this for your talk with Frank." Lauren wriggled her eyebrows. "Know what I mean?"

"Does it have to be lingerie? Couldn't it be shoes? Or another haircut? How about scarves? There are some really extravagant silk scarves out there. Cashmere pashimas? How about—"

"Alice, we are not treating ourselves to scarves or cashmere pashimas. That's for grandmothers and great-aunts!" Realizing her friend already qualified for one of those titles, she added, "Old-fashioned grandmothers and great-aunts. We're going for lingerie, the sexier, the better."

Douce Flagrance was the sort of place men came to buy presents for women. Charles might have come here to pick up gifts for Tracie. He certainly hadn't made any stops for Lauren. Their sex life, after the children were born, had soon become as boring and lusterless as the rest of their relationship.

Forget Charles. This wasn't about him. This was about her and wanting courage to help her through to-night's date.

Michael Connolly was a science writer who was also represented by Louise, a literary agent who thought her professional duties occasionally extended to her clients' personal lives. Louise had been trying to hook up Lauren and Michael for a while. Despite the fiasco of her last date with Andrew Rose, Lauren had finally given in. How could she encourage her readers to enjoy their single state, if she wasn't willing to do that herself?

She trailed her hand against a silk camisole. It felt soft—the way she would like to feel again. It had been a long time since she had ventured into a place like this. She hadn't indulged in feminine frills or enjoyed the caress of soft fabric against her skin in decades. Quite simply, she had settled into a routine. You choose your husband and your lingerie and you stick with them, until divorce do you part. So now, more than a year after her divorce decree had come through, she was ready to proudly proclaim: off with the old bra and on with the new!

Lauren fingered the smooth camisole fringed with lace.

"A woman's choice," said the shop assistant, who Clare had introduced as Estelle. "Men are visual, they prefer something see-through. Women notice texture."

Estelle probably knew everything there was to know about the differences between the sexes when shopping for garments that inspired the art of seduction.

Lauren pulled a lace-up merry widow off the rack and tried to imagine herself in it. She couldn't.

"Would you like to see that in your size?" Estelle asked.

"Uh, no. I don't think it's me."

Estelle nodded. She crossed the room, but was back in a minute with Clare close behind her. "What about this bra?"

Lauren stared at the wisp of soft tissue-like fabric that had been pushed in her hand. "It's pink. I can't wear pink."

Clare looked up. "Why not? Under your clothes it doesn't matter. Nobody's going to know anyway. And you should listen to people who know more than you."

"I thought sexy lingerie was a woman's secret power tool," Lauren muttered under her breath. "Some power I have here!"

Although Estelle was loyal to Clare, a frequent, long-established customer, she was clever enough not to want to alienate a new shopper. She reached for a black push-up bra and offered it to Lauren, who promptly rejected it, as well as the floral red bra that followed.

"And forget anything demi," Lauren told the clerk. "I'm not planning on showing any cleavage."

"Clare, *cherie*," Estelle said in what didn't sound anything like a French accent. "Your friend is not being very cooperative. Does she want my help or not?"

"Lauren! Behave!" Clare shouted from across the room, where she'd gone to help Alice by pulling a beige full-coverage bra away from her. "No. No. No. Forget that. We want sexy, not practical and menopausal."

Peering over Clare's shoulder, Alice gave Lauren a little shrug and moved to the displays of teddies, bustiers and other corsetlike contraptions that looked very useful for bondage. Clare pulled something off the rack and pushed Alice into a changing room.

Lauren soon followed, after settling for a black bra with much more lace than she had ever seen. It shimmered against her skin, holding up her breasts quite gently. It was more low cut than the style she usually favored, revealing more cleavage, but it was not bad from the front. She twisted her head. Not bad from the back. She turned to see herself in profile.

Okay, don't look too close. The point is to feel good rather than look good because, as Clare had reminded her, nobody was going to look—especially not her date. But if the bra gave her even the tiniest drop of courage to survive the next few hours with a perfect stranger, it was worth it.

"I'll get it," Lauren announced as she stepped out of the dressing room. "Now, what about a camisole? And matching panties? I see you have sleepwear, too."

It was a while before Lauren handed her credit card to Estelle and paid for her purchases, which included something special for Helen.

"Thank you for your help," she said with a smile that was sincere. "I'll think of you when I wear them tonight."

Clare twirled around. "Tonight?"

"I'm going on a date." Lauren exchanged glances with Alice. "Didn't I mention it?"

"Well, here I was hoping for a girls' night out," Clare said to Alice after Lauren had left them. "What about you? Are you up for something?"

"I think I'd better go home." Alice patted the elegant shopping bag in her hand. "There's a conversation that's long overdue."

"Okay. Maybe another time."

Clare waved goodbye to Alice and contemplated where to go. The thought of returning to her empty apartment was not appealing. She would be better off heading for her office. Although, for once, she was caught up with all of her work.

Maybe there was a movie she could go to. Or maybe she could treat herself to a meal at Jamal's or Chez Vartan the same way she had splurged on that silk camisole. It beat holding her breath waiting for some-one else to take her, because there simply wasn't anyone these days.

Well, actually, there was someone, only she wasn't sure she had his number—or that she should call him.

"Well, that was very nice." Michael Connolly joined Lauren and the rest of the audience in giving a final round of applause to the author who had just completed a reading from his latest book. "I'm glad you suggested it. I've read most of Trusser's books, but I've never heard him read before. It changes things a bit. I'll know what to look for next time I pick up one of his works."

"I'm glad you liked it." Lauren smiled politely. "He's a natural performer, almost as much as he's a storyteller."

"So much so that I could kill him out of pure jeal-ousy." Michael grinned, adding warmth to what Lauren had originally deemed to be cold, steel-blue eyes. "If I didn't like his work so much."

"From what I understand you have nothing to worry about."

That was Louise's claim. She had raved so much about Michael Connolly's work that Lauren had picked up some of it, even though she usually preferred not to read contemporary material when she was in the middle of her own writing. When she found his second book to be even better than his first—both of which she had finished in one sitting—she realized once again why she had that rule. There was nothing like someone else's creative accomplishments to make you realize how far you had to go! Because Michael Connolly's humorous but clarifying accounts of the upcoming nanotech revolution added another three hundred miles to her already tortuous route, a journey that her divorce, writer's block, job search and singles column had already significantly prolonged.

It was Michael's writing that had finally convinced her to go on the date with him. She didn't expect much. Her last date had left her wary. But since then, she had armed herself with wisdom about taking the pressure off the first date. She could recite the information she'd gathered for her column with her eyes closed: five dress tips for making a first impression; four places to go; three topics NOT to bring up; two easy ways out of a disaster; one essential thing never to forget—have fun.

Lauren had decided that the only way she was going to have fun was by doing something that would steer attention away from herself and her date, such as visiting her favorite community bookstore to hear a book reading. That way, if Michael Connolly complained about his ex-wife or ogled younger women, Lauren would have other, more entertaining distractions. That way, the evening wouldn't be a total waste of time.

And if he didn't have those shortcomings, the two of them would have a ready-made subject to discuss that would steer them away from themselves and the ghosts of their pasts. She hadn't exactly had her writing in mind, though.

"Every professional writer has something to worry about," Michael was saying. "If it's not writer's block, then it's sales figures or computer viruses or editorial changes you just don't want to make. I'm sure you know the routine."

Tossing his head slightly and shaking his blondish hair, Michael gave her a conspiratorial wink.

"I do, but I'm sure Tony Trusser doesn't." Lauren tilted her head toward the man on the podium, now surrounded by fans offering him gratitude and adulation. "Do you want to meet him?"

"By the looks of the line that's forming, we'd have to wait forever. Wouldn't you rather get something at the café instead? I'd like to hear what you think about those odd images he uses."

Lauren hesitated for a second. She had her exit line ready and could leave if she wanted. But the café within the bookstore was hardly a high-pressure venue for a first date, and she and Michael did have something to talk about, even if it reminded her a bit too much of her own pressing deadlines.

Then, of course, there was Michael Connolly with his steel-blue eyes and his dirty blond hair. He was taller than Charles, and his shoulders were definitely broader. Much broader than those she would associate with a middle-aged science writer, more like those belonging to an athlete. Although telltale signs of age marked his face, he seemed to keep his body in shape. Lauren had noticed that during the reading, when her eyes had occasionally wandered to his corduroy-clad limbs next to her. She had immediately reined in her interest, blaming her uncharacteristic behavior on her bra; nothing like new clothes to bring back old desires.

It had been a while since Lauren had paid enough attention to a man to notice his limbs. Her attraction to Charles had died a long time ago, and anything she had felt for him during the last few years of their marriage had been more from habit and familiarity than anything else. She had thought her dulled senses were due to her age. So why was she so aware of this man sitting next to her? What was this peculiar and much-forgotten tingly feeling in her stomach?

Tingly? She hadn't really thought "tingly," had she? She must be letting her column get to her, if she was using such romantic, youthful vocabulary. She accepted

Michael's invitation in the prim and polite words of the fifty-something she was.

Despite the crowd at the reading, it wasn't hard to find a table at the café, and they didn't have to wait too long for the waitress to bring their drinks. Lauren insisted on paying for her own. To her surprise, Michael didn't object.

"Bet you weren't expecting that!" he said, grinning. "I learned the hard way."

"Lost your fingers the first time you tried?"

"Something like that. When I first started dating after my, um, divorce, I made a lot of noises about paying. It's what I used to do, way back in the Jurassic era. Anyway, to make a long story short, my kids set me straight. Who would have thought they would be teaching me?"

"I know what you mean," Lauren said, thinking of everything she had learned over the past few weeks from young people. "So now you know all the rules?"

"That would be the day! But I know enough to know that I've just broken another one. Don't talk about your exploits. So about that imagery…"

They discussed Trusser's work, comparing it with their own projects occasionally. To her surprise, Lauren found herself confessing how slowly she had been advancing with her manuscript. Michael admitted that he had had similar problems. He mentioned techniques he had developed during his slumps.

Lauren tried to concentrate, but she could feel one of the straps from her bra sliding off her shoulder. She had adjusted it earlier, but apparently she hadn't found the correct length yet. That was the problem with new clothes—it took a while to break them in. She wriggled uncomfortably, waiting for a moment when Michael would turn away so she could pull the strap up again.

"This is a bit awkward," he said, a strange tone in his voice that made Lauren think he was going to offer her a tip about the bra strap. She straightened, a polite smile frozen on her face as she waited for him to continue. "It's been bothering me all evening so I'm going to go ahead and ask."

"Oh-kay," she said, hoping to convey her reluctance. She tried to ignore the way the fallen strap was cutting into her shoulder.

"You weren't married to Charles Gard by any chance?"

Lauren forgot about the bra strap.

"Actually I was," she said slowly, wondering what was coming next.

"I know him. I used to work with him. Well, not with him. I did some freelancing for him."

Although a number of thoughts flooded her brain, Lauren could think of nothing to say that would have passed as acceptable first date banter. She looked down at her mocha-latte.

"I probably shouldn't have brought it up," he said,

after a moment. "But I thought I'd better be up front. In case we decide to see each other again." He paused.

Lauren kept her eyes on her latte, desperately trying to come up with some response.

"Of course, with what I've just said," he continued with a self-conscious laugh, "you probably don't want to see me again. You probably want to leave right away."

"No, not right away," she said, looking over his shoulder at the book display behind him. "I would like to finish my drink first."

She emptied her cup immediately.

"I still don't feel completely comfortable when I come here," Anton Muller said, as he and Clare made their way past the bars, bistros and theaters on North Clark Street. He waved his arms at the activity around them. "I know all this gentrification gave new life to an old neighborhood, but sometimes I miss the old one—with all its problems." He grinned down at her. "I guess *you* wouldn't know about *those*."

"You'd be surprised," Clare mumbled before she realized what she was revealing.

"Okay. Surprise me."

Clare could feel her face flushing under Anton's close scrutiny. Earlier after some reflection, she had finally decided to see if Anton wanted to join her for dinner. Nothing wrong with a meal between colleagues, she told herself. Besides, they did have a case or two to discuss, and he probably would have something else lined up anyway.

As it turned out, he didn't, and he had other ideas of what they could do. He had suggested trying some of Chicago's world-famous improvisational theater. So instead of an *haute cuisine* French meal, they had gone to a Thai fast-food joint before heading to a performance.

As they worked their way through the noodles, their business connection hadn't come up once. Instead, Clare had discovered that they both liked pulp fiction from the thirties and political thrillers from the fifties, and that Anton was a real aficionado of independent rock music. Now she was learning that he had grown up in Wrigley Park and, as a boy, had witnessed the neighborhood's urban renewal. His experience encouraged her to open up about her past.

"I grew up in Queens, New York. A regular Mediterranean melting pot in those days."

"Mediterranean? With a name like Hanley?"

"My mother came from Cyprus. Her accent was so thick, sometimes even I couldn't understand her."

"So you're Greek, huh?" He held up both hands, palms up. "Don't tell me. Hanley is English for Hanlipolou or Hanlidis?"

Clare worked on her lips to suppress her laughter, then she tilted her head back to look at him. "No. Hanley is my father's name. He was never a serious part of my life."

He had always been too drunk for that. The only thing she remembered about him was his smell, a distinctive blend of alcohol, cigarettes and sweat. Then one day, he wasn't there anymore, and she never missed him.

"So you owe everything to your mother?"

"Absolutely everything." They pushed their way past a long line waiting outside a famous dinner theater. "It's amazing really, when I think about it. She was pretty close to being illiterate, but being Greek, she knew the value of learning, so she made me learn. Boy, did she make me!" Clare rolled her eyes. "When all the other kids in the neighborhood were going for afternoon jobs, my mother worked extra shifts at a pizza place to pay for my tutoring. I hated it then, but it got me a scholarship to college and well, here I am." She opened her arms wide, then dropped them to her sides.

"I guess that's something else we have in common. A single mother."

"Your father left?"

"Yes. I, uh, kicked him out when I was fifteen. I wasn't going to let him knock down a woman half his size."

"You—" She stopped suddenly, and he halted, too. "But you couldn't have been much bigger yourself?"

"I was sober. That helped. And no one else would do it, no one else would make him stop, except for one guy, a cop."

Anton's face was hidden in the shadows, but Clare saw him now as she had never seen him before. Overwhelmed and impressed, she continued their slow pace up the street.

"Is that why you joined the force?"

He nodded. "We weren't supposed to like cops too much in the old neighborhood, but you know what? This man was the only person besides me who ever stood between my father's fists and my mother's face. I didn't realize how much he risked for himself until I was called in on a 'domestic disturbance.'" From Anton's tone, Clare could tell how little he approved of the euphemism. "It's strange how everyone talks about dangerous criminals and violent gangs. But the only time I was ever hurt in the line of duty was when I was trying to get a gun away from a drunk who didn't like the *pelecinke* his wife had cooked. Funny, isn't it?" He laughed without humor.

"Is that why you left? The force, I mean."

"Partly. I was going nowhere and I thought I could do something more in another branch of the law. And I guess, I wanted to do my mother proud. Real proud, I mean."

"I understand. I wish my mother could have seen me graduate from law school. She died before I finished," Clare added in response to the inquisitive glance he shot her.

"So you're all alone?"

"Pretty much. I have cousins in Queens and some back in Cyprus, but I'm not very close to any of them."

She wasn't close to anyone, really. With the exception of Lauren and Alice and a few other friends, her work had been her life. It had never really bothered her. But now, she wondered whether she could have something else, something more. How different would things be with someone who could really share her life?

Clare looked around at the crowd moving around them. She told herself to stop her girlish dreams and to remember her middle-aged realities. She couldn't take a chance on Anton. At least, not yet, not until after the Van Belden account was settled. Just being here with him tonight was a big risk. Despite Lauren and Alice's encouragement the other night and the intimacy of her and Anton's conversation—or maybe because of it, Clare couldn't shake her doubts that they should be here together.

"Anton, this is a bit awkward, but..." She stopped, embarrassed to go on. After several seconds, she swallowed, clearing her throat and continued, "I was going to say this earlier, but I guess we were talking so intently that I forgot. I..."

Again she stopped.

He didn't say anything. His eyes focused on her, his face expressionless, waiting for her to speak.

"I think it would be better if we didn't publicize our friendship," she said, choosing her words carefully, "I mean, I know our going out together like this doesn't mean anything. There's nothing wrong with it. But I wouldn't want people to think that you...that I...that you and I, you know. Not with the Van Belden decision coming up. You understand, don't you?"

"I'm not sure I do, Clare, but if you're asking me not to mention being here with you tonight, I won't."

He bent his head to examine something on his sleeve, then looked back at her. "I'm not saying that I agree with you on this. There's nothing wrong with us being here together."

Clare took a moment to watch a couple strolling past them. Then, she continued, "You're right. There's nothing to be ashamed of. But you can't imagine what people will say, especially where a big account and a lot of money are concerned."

"I don't—"

"Believe me. I know."

Anton studied her closely and, despite the darkness, Clare felt he could see into her soul.

"Okay," he said after a long moment. "If that's what you want."

"It is." Clare felt her whole body sighing with relief. "So now that that's settled, let go see some improv. I didn't invite you out to stand here all night."

CHAPTER 12

"So what do you think? Is the coding okay or do I need to reprogram the whole thing again?" Helen asked Joe Bardet.

He had complained about a program he couldn't master, and she had been happy to help out, stopping by his office to take a look.

Now, she made a couple more changes, then ran the program again. When everything seemed to be all right, she swiveled her chair around. "Looks like it's going to be okay."

"Wow! You make it seem so easy. Now I really feel like an idiot."

"No, don't feel that way," Helen said, more alarmed about how she was making him feel than about blowing her cover. "It's a common mistake. I know because I make it all the time. I mean, I used to when I was programming."

Helen didn't wait to hear Joe's answer. She turned back to the computer, pretending to check the program again while Joe rolled his chair closer so he could see the printout. When she swiveled again, she wasn't expecting him to be close enough for her to inhale his scent, feel the heat of his body and see the fullness of his mouth and the redness of his lips. She wasn't expecting to shake her head slowly, as if she were saying "No" to temptation, only to be flooded by that temptation. She wasn't expecting to brush his lips with hers. Just once. But—oh, God!—once was enough.

She wanted more. She wanted to press her mouth fully against his. She wanted him to shower little kisses over her cheeks, eyes, neck and then her lips again. She wanted him to whisper her name in a voice hoarse with desire. She wanted—

No. Forget it. Stop. She rolled her chair away from him and saw that he was looking at her with what might be a meaningful gaze, a gaze that said everything she wanted to say and couldn't.

Mortified, Helen swiveled back toward the computer and counted to ten, then turned her attention to the printout in front of her, seeking comfort in what she did best—programming.

"There," she said in a voice that sounded almost normal, only a little strained. "There. That's where the problem was. You have to change these numbers around and then it works. Okay?"

She looked at him, making sure their faces didn't meet and their lips didn't brush and...

"Okay," he said, sounding like it wasn't, sounding like he was asking a question rather than answering one.

"Okay." She had no idea what she was agreeing to, except that it had nothing to do with programming.

Joe seemed to be about to say something, but shrugged instead. Then, he turned to the printout on the table as if nothing had happened.

Nothing was ever going to happen. It couldn't. And wasn't that a shame. Here she was as Lauren, Queen of the Chicago Single Chicks, and she was still being treated like computer geek Helen. Clothes really didn't make the woman after all. In the end, every guy, including Joe, wanted only one thing from her: her brain.

She wanted to cry from desperation, to scream with frustration, but she managed to contain herself, until they were packing to leave.

"So, Lauren, what is the difference between boy shorts and bikinis?"

"The sex who wears them?" Helen answered, not sure whether it was a joke or if she wanted to discuss intimate apparel with him.

"The sex who wears them? You don't really expect me to laugh at that. Come on, you can do better. Tell me the difference. My sisters don't know. Apparently, it's not something that comes up a lot in *Cosmo*. They asked me to ask you, after they read last week's column."

"Oh, that!" Helen said, as if she'd understood all the time, as if she actually knew the answer. She had only skimmed Lauren's column. She hadn't memorized it.

Why should she? She hadn't known that Joe would be quizzing her on it.

The only boy shorts she had in mind were his. Truth be told, she didn't have his shorts in mind, at all; more like his bare butt. She pretended to fiddle with the printout sheets so he wouldn't catch her blush.

"Yes, *that*," he said. "I don't really care. I don't think most guys do unless they're buying something for their, um, girlfriend. I'm just asking for my sisters."

He actually sounded embarrassed. Why he would be, she didn't know. Maybe because of that lip brush that had happened earlier, or more likely because he didn't want to talk about women's underwear, especially not his sisters' underwear.

"So, what *is* the difference between boy shorts and bikinis?" Joe repeated.

"Boy shorts and bikinis?"

"Yes."

"The difference between boy shorts and bikinis is…"

"Yes?"

"Well boy shorts are…" Helen exhaled.

Come on, Helen. Think. It can't be that complicated. You can write computer programs that could probably design underwear and mass produce it, as well. Surely, you can figure out the difference between shorts and bikinis.

Wait a minute. What kind of lingerie had Lauren given her? They looked like shorts, but you never knew when it came to lingerie. Maybe they were bikinis, after all.

"You don't have to tell me, if you don't want to. I understand," Joe said, with such a nice smile that Helen was certain he meant it. Because of that, she felt she had to give him an answer, any answer, even a bad answer, even the wrong answer, even a blatant lie. He would never know the difference anyway.

"Boy shorts are, you know, like shorts boys wear. And bikinis are, you know, like bikinis. They only come up to here." She drew a line near her hips. She exaggerated her strokes so she looked like she knew what she was drawing, but the position of the line was vague enough so he couldn't call her bluff.

Joe gave her a funny look. "I'm sorry. You'll have to do that again. I didn't get it."

Helen scowled and sighed loudly. Maybe he would withdraw his question.

He didn't.

She went for diversion. "Oh, my God, did you see what time it is? I really have to go…"

"But Lauren…"

"Maybe some other time," Helen said over her shoulder as she dashed out of the room as quickly as her high heels would carry her.

Helen was glad the lights were out when she arrived home. She wasn't ready for a tea-and-tell with Lauren, who had probably gone out with her friend Alice again. It was only when Helen stepped into the kitchen that she realized the lights didn't shine through the closed doors. Lauren, Alice and Clare were in the breakfast room. Helen hoped to say hello and sneak away, but the three other women weren't having it.

"Come have some wine with us." Lauren patted the chair next to her.

Helen joined them at the table.

"We were just talking about how lingerie doesn't seem to be a magic answer for romance. All of us have tried it, and it didn't work."

"Not for me, either," Helen admitted and told them how Joe's interest in the subject had almost unveiled their conspiracy. "It was, like, so embarrassing."

"Embarrassing? You should be flattered. I am. He read the column, Helen." Lauren smiled. "Now, why do I think that's because of you?"

Helen sipped at her more wine to cover her blush. With hands that were almost trembling, she put her glass down. Then, fortified by the sudden rush of alcohol, she raised both hands. "I was, like, *difference?* What difference?"

"At least he knows shorts and bikinis are different," Alice said.

Helen had no idea how much wine Alice had consumed, but it looked as if she'd had quite a hit. It was obviously taking a lot for her to sound so cheerful. "I don't think Frank notices anything. He just doesn't care anymore."

"Have you tried to talk to him?" Clare asked.

"I've tried."

"And?"

"He walked away." Alice's head rested on her arms on the table. "How can you talk to somebody who doesn't want to talk to you, who's more interested in looking at the women in the infomercials than at you in your new, lace fringed camisole?"

"Strutting around in an enticing camisole isn't exactly my idea of establishing communication lines," Clare said.

Helen knew things were really bad when Alice barely lifted up her head to answer. "What do you suggest?"

Clare shrugged. "I don't know."

"Counseling." Lauren put her glass down. "Marriage counseling. Have you considered that?"

The shake of Alice's head was barely perceptible. "I can't get him to sit in the same room with me. How am I going to get him to a counselor?"

"You could always kidnap him. Tie him down." Clare rolled her fingers in the air to show exactly how it could be done. "And force him to listen to you."

"Why, Clare," Lauren said, "I always thought you were a nonviolent person."

"If she's not, I am," Alice interjected with sudden energy. "Anyway, it's too late for that. I did the next best thing. I moved out." She smiled gratefully at Lauren. "He knows where he can get me. If he wants to."

"And if he doesn't?"

"I guess I'll be able to deal with it. I'm in good company, here at Lauren's Singles Hotel."

Lauren got up and walked into the kitchen. She had been hearing the steady dripping of water from the kitchen sink. Helen must not have turned it off all the way. She gave the tap a twist, then returned to the break-fast room, where Clare was still interrogating Alice.

"Has Frank been in touch since then?"

Alice looked at Lauren, who shrugged her shoulders and answered for Alice. "Apparently not."

"So the battle lines are drawn?" Clare asked.

"You could say that. The way I figure it, it's Frank's move. I've told him that I want something other than this. I've tried to show him I care. Now it's up to him. More wine, anyone?"

Alice raised the bottle, tilting it in the direction of each of the women around the table. Helen and Clare declined, while Lauren pushed her glass forward. Alice poured. She didn't refill her own glass; it was still almost full.

"So, no, Lauren," she said. "Lingerie was not the magic answer. Not in my case, anyway."

"Well, I don't think it was a complete failure in mine," Clare said. "I had a very nice time with Anton. He's thoughtful and generous and very good company."

"And you're going to see him again?" Lauren asked.

"Of course, I am. We work together."

Lauren flung her arms in the air. They made a loud plop as they fell back into her lap. "That's not what I meant, and you know it. So are you?"

Clare studied her manicured fingers. "Quite honestly, I don't know. I'm not sure it's right, and that it won't cause problems."

"But you want to?"

"Yes," Clare said slowly as if just saying the word took effort. "Yes, I think I do."

"I knew it!" Lauren gleamed triumphantly at Alice. "I knew it! That's great, Clare. That's *really* great."

Clare wrinkled her brow. "It's complicated."

"But you talked to him? You discussed your feelings about the office conflict?"

"Yes. I suggested we be discreet about our friendship, at least for the moment."

"I suppose that's a good idea." Lauren glanced at Alice, then back at Clare. "I'm glad you came clean. Talking things out is always important."

Lauren was focused on Clare, so almost didn't catch Helen's moan. She glanced at her quickly and was surprised to see color creeping up Helen's pale features. This talk about coming clean couldn't mean anything to her. She couldn't be seriously interested in Joe, could she?

"Look who's talking," Clare said. "Look what honesty got you! Who would have guessed your date knew Charles?"

"That was strange," Lauren agreed.

"I guess that means you're not going to see him again."

Lauren shook her head slowly. "I don't think so. It's too strange."

"But you said he was nice," Helen said, any telltale signs of her emotions now gone. "And he inspired you to start working on your book again. What else do you want?"

"Severing the connection with Charles would be on the top of my list," Lauren said, acknowledging why Michael Connolly's admission had disturbed her so much.

"Oh, come on." Clare drummed her nails against the table. "You're not going to let Charles get in your way again. It's not like they're close friends or anything. They worked together once. I bet they never crossed paths since."

"It's not Charles, it's me. I don't think I'm ready for anything serious yet. I need more time with myself before I get involved with anyone. Who knows? Maybe it's time I tried the single life."

"Try it? I thought you were already doing more than that."

"No, I've just been going through the motions," Lauren said. "Now I'm ready for the real thing."

"Hey, Mom!" Chrissie's cheerful voice came through the receiver. "It's been a while since we talked. Are you so busy being a hot single chick you don't have the time to talk to your daughter?"

"Chrissie! How are you?!" Lauren said, far too happy

to be speaking to her daughter to be annoyed with her teasing. When she thought about it, it was true that she had been too busy lately to call her daughter, not that she missed her any less.

Lauren settled comfortably into her leather armchair, while she and Chrissie chatted. Chrissie reported on the politics going on at her office and then gave her mother a detailed account of a recent party she had attended, held in an eighteenth-century country mansion. In turn, Lauren filled in her daughter on all the developments in her life that she hadn't mentioned in her e-mails.

"So you're working on the book again?" Chrissie asked.

"Yes, I am. The first draft is almost done now. Of course, there will be a lot of revisions. But the book is getting there."

"That's great, Mom."

"Mmm. I think so, too."

"And the column?"

"Keeps me on my toes."

"That's good."

It would be, except that there was something in Helen's reaction the other night that had disturbed Lauren and made her question the cost of her success.

"Actually, Chrissie, I'm concerned about Helen."

"Helen? She sounds happy."

"No, you don't understand. I think she likes Joe, the Web designer. But now that I've drawn her into my, um, tangled web, she can't tell him the truth about who she is."

"You didn't draw her into anything. She stepped right in."

"With a little push."

"She's a big girl, Mom. She'll figure something out."

"That's what I'm worried about. That she'll figure out the wrong thing."

"Helen is brilliant. She doesn't do wrong."

"She may when it comes to men. I'm afraid she'll give Joe up because of me. You know, like in the Cyrano de Bergerac story. Remember? The hero thinks he's too old and ugly to win the girl, so he writes the love letters for his friend instead, and in the end, no one is happy."

"Of course not, they all die, but that's not going to happen here." Chrissie sighed impatiently. "And that story is so Old World, so tragic and dramatic. Besides, in that story it's the writer who gives up the girl. That would be you and, somehow, I don't think you're interested in Joe."

"No, but I care about Helen. I don't want to spoil her chance."

"Mom, if it weren't for you, Helen wouldn't have had a chance with Joe. Would you want her to tell him the truth?"

Lauren didn't hesitate. "If it mattered to her."

"But you don't know that it does, do you, Mom? Has she said anything?"

"No, not exactly. But I can tell. She gets flustered when she's going to meet him. She's tongue-tied when he calls." Lauren didn't bother to mention how strangely Helen had behaved the other night, after being with Joe.

"Mom, that's Helen. She's always been timid. Don't worry about it."

Lauren tried again. "Chrissie, I can't stand in the way of her happiness."

Chrissie made a funny coughing noise that sounded like she could be laughing. "Her happiness? Aren't you making too big a deal out of this? Helen and Joe just met."

"But, Chrissie, don't you see? Even if Helen does tell Joe the truth now, will he still want to have anything to do with her? She lied to him. Who likes that?"

"Forget it, Mom. Don't get involved. It's Helen's decision."

Lauren dropped the subject, knowing she and Chrissie wouldn't see eye-to-eye. But she would deal with the problem, sooner or later, even if Chrissie didn't agree.

She turned to a less thorny topic. "I told you Alice moved in?"

"Yes, you did. How's she holding up?"

"She doesn't break into tears every five minutes, but she's not doing too well."

"She must miss Frank. Are they going to, um, you know, um…"

"To divorce? It's okay. You can say it, sweetheart. I'm fine." And it didn't even surprise Lauren to realize she was. "And, no, I don't think so. Alice and Frank love each other. They just need some time apart to think things through."

Lauren really hoped that that was the case. When her friend had arrived on her doorstep, she had welcomed her with open arms. How could she do otherwise after all the hand-holding and comforting Alice had given her in the past? But that hadn't stopped Lauren from worrying about the outcome, that Alice's departure would be forever, that Frank would take her temporary retreat for permanent withdrawal.

But for all Lauren's worries, she admired her friend for confronting her marital problems. Unlike Alice, Lauren had refused to admit that her marriage had been falling apart. She couldn't acknowledge the marriage was over until Charles had left her for Tracie.

"And how are you dealing with roommates?" Chrissie asked.

"It's like having a family again."

And it was, Lauren reflected after she hung up. Because like singles, families came in all sizes and shapes. Two months ago, her world had been so dark, she couldn't see past her bed. Now, she hadn't finished her book, but she was getting there. She hadn't dealt with all her financial problems, but thanks to the money from the column and rent from Helen, she had saved the house from an imminent sale. Most importantly, she was actually enjoying the single life.

All of this she owed to her friends. For months she had been totally overwhelmed by her own miseries, she hadn't seen the crises in their lives. It was time to pay her debt. Time to do something for them.

To: sherelle@chicgazette.com
From: lauren@onsurf.com
Subject: 50+
Hey Sherelle,
Have a great new direction I would like to explore in upcoming columns—the fifty-plus singles scene. Readers are asking for it. I'm dying to look into it. Before I'm too old! What do you think?
Lauren

To: lauren@onsurf.com
From: sherelle@chicgazette.com
Subject: Re: 50+
hey lauren. good of you to check with me first. interesting possibility, but do you really think you can deal with the subject? not really your expertise. we already have our midlife expert—kyle—and wouldn't want the overlap with her column.—s

To: sherelle@chicgazette.com
From: lauren@onsurf.com
Subject: Re: 50+
Hey again. Sorry to say this, but readers DO want to hear about it (see attached mails). They can't all be wrong. Can we ask them to write in? Maybe share their experiences? I don't think kyle's touched on it yet.—L.

To: lauren@onsurf.com
From: sherelle@chicgazette.com
Subject: Re: 50+
lauren—will check with kyle and let you know, but quite honestly, am not hot for it. let's stick with something we know, and leave the oldies to the oldies.—s

To: sherelle@chicgazette.com
From: lauren@onsurf.com
Subject: Re: 50+
Hey Sherelle,
Okay, so maybe I don't know much about it, but I do know somebody who does. We could write it together. Or she could be a guest columnist. What do you think?—L.

To: lauren@onsurf.com
From: sherelle@chicgazette.com
Subject: Re: 50+
kyle would be furious if we went over her head on this one. stick to your usual plz.—s

To: sherelle@chicgazette.com
From: lauren@onsurf.com
Subject: Re: 50+
Me again. Same record, same song, new riff.
Did you know that midlife singles form a significant portion of the single population—one that is underexamined when compared to their twenty- and thirty-year-old counterparts? If this sounds like sociologese, it's because I'm quoting a report from the

Third Age Society. The report includes statistics about their sex life (yes, they have one). Aren't you curious?—L.

To: lauren@onsurf.com
From: sherelle@chicgazette.com
Subject: Re: 50+
Lauren—am curious. but not enough to ok a column. would be kind of like hearing how my parents make out. am so not ready for that! hey, shouldn't you be writing your column instead of playing old tunes? am clearing time tomorrow so i can read it.
btw don't forget the heart-to-heart benefit. coming up soon. great showcase for you and the paper. c u there, i hope.—s

So that was it. No oldies.

Every instinct Lauren had was telling her this topic was hot. Baby Boomers dating again? The first time they had been at it they had revolutionized sexuality. This time round they would revolutionize old age. Lauren was dying to write the story, and not just because she wanted a way out for Helen and Joe.

But Sherelle said no. What kind of an editor did that make her? Especially if she didn't want to face some home truths like hearing how her parents made out. How did she think she got here in the first place?

The only kind of oldies Sherelle seemed not to mind were the ones who would show up for the heart disease

benefit the newspaper was cosponsoring. But when it
came to the hearts of older singles, forget it!

Lauren couldn't forget it, though. This could have
been her ticket out. This could have been the way to
introduce herself as the real Lauren and to clear things
up between Joe and Helen before it was too late.

But if Sherelle wouldn't let her write about baby
boomers, how would she ever accept one as a columnist? Helen would just have to go on pretending to be
Lauren for a while longer, and Lauren would have to
think of another way to sort things out.

CHAPTER 13

"Is there anything else we need to discuss?" Clare leaned back in her chair and eyed the three men at the table. She hoped the debriefing would be over soon because she didn't have anything more to contribute. Her mind was already elsewhere, and she wanted to get the rest of her there, too.

She was going to invite Anton to go with her to the *Chicago Gazette*'s Heart-to-Heart Benefit. She had been avoiding him ever since their last outing. But after talking it out with her friends and thinking about it on her own, she had finally decided that Anton was worth a try. Clare was also determined to do it right this time: no sleazy hideaways, no slinking around. She and Anton were unattached, consenting adults. They didn't have anything to be ashamed of. The office gossips might not think so, and the "boys" might not approve, but, in the end, they didn't matter. Only Anton and she did.

"Well, if that's all there is, I hope you gentlemen will excuse me," she said now to her male colleagues, pushing back her chair. She was almost at her office when she noticed Robert Brooks following her.

"Do you think I could have a word with you in private?"

Without waiting for her to answer, he followed her into her office and shut the door behind them. Had he been anyone else, Clare would have shown him straight out. But Robert was one of the few senior colleagues who genuinely appreciated and respected her work. In a pinch, he would close ranks on her as quickly and as tightly as he would on any outsider. The rest of the time, he treated her better than most. For that, she sometimes overlooked his condescension.

Clare leaned against the table, her feet slightly apart, her arms crossed in front of her chest. "What can I do for you, Robert?"

"It has been mentioned that you are seeing a lot of Anton Muller."

"We're working on a number of cases together." Clare met Robert's eyes. She could imagine where this was going, and she didn't want him to think she was hiding anything. "He's a very good lawyer, and his help is invaluable."

"You know he is short-listed to take over the Van Belden account?"

"I know. I've been examining all the candidates very closely. I'll be making my recommendations next week." She bent her head to flick a speck off her skirt. "He would be a good choice."

"And you base your conclusion on...?"

"The quality of his work, his perseverance, his dedication, his thoroughness. All the things I consider in any staffing decisions."

"You are certain that nothing else is affecting your judgment?"

"Of course not."

"That's not what everyone else is saying."

"Robert, I don't have time to listen to what everyone says." Her arms tightened as she held back her growing anger. She smiled. "I'm surprised you do."

He didn't smile back. "It's even being said that he's counting on your recommendation, expecting it, especially now that the two of you seem to be an item."

Astounded by how much the office gossips had surmised and by how poorly informed they were, Clare didn't flinch. "Let them say what they want. I know a good lawyer when I see one."

"Yes, you do, Clare. You certainly do. You've never made a bad call yet. Still—"

"You can count on me to offer my best judgment."

Clare's words came out with a conviction that surprised her. Inside she was stuttering, blabbering, dithering. What? Not possible. How did they know? Did he talk? If he did, then why? How could he? No way. No possible way.

She waited for Robert to leave. Then she sank into

her chair to make sense of the voices echoing in the theater of her mind.

She had to face the facts. Despite her request, Anton had talked about them. How else could anyone have known they were "an item"? Worse, he had been playing her all along! No wonder she had been running into him so often lately! It had been part of his carefully orchestrated plan to get to her and to the Van Belden account. He'd almost won. She'd almost believed he really cared. She'd almost been taken in again.

But, she reminded herself, all her encounters with Anton had been spontaneous and coincidental—except for the ones she'd planned. The evidence for a conspiracy just wasn't there. She was reading into it, listening to the gossips instead of her instincts.

Instincts? She should know better than to listen to them after the last time. They'd done much more damage than any gossip. Maybe those spontaneous encounters weren't so spontaneous, after all.

Impossible! There was no way Anton could have known where she was meeting her blind date and she would be stood up, no way Anton could have found out about the music clubs. It just wasn't possible.

Robert and the gossips were wrong. Anton really did care about her; it wasn't just about getting the account. He had been kind, gentle and thoughtful. He had never pushed when she had said no. He'd understood her qualms, although he'd questioned her insistence on waiting until after the Van Belden decision.

There was only one thing to do, Clare decided. She would have to ask him, and he would have to choose.

"I thought you would still be here," Anton said, popping his head in the doorway an hour later. "Mind if I come in?"

"Not at all." Clare put her pen down, stacked her papers and leaned back in her chair. "Please do."

"I was wondering whether I could drag you away. Maybe get a bite to eat. It's probably too late for some more improv, but it's never too late to dine. In fact, a friend of mine just opened a restaurant. I thought you might like to try it."

The words came out quickly, as if he were nervous, which, of course, he would be if he suspected she was on to him.

"Or we could try something else, if you prefer. If you don't have any other plans, that is," he went on, with his boyish grin, making her wish she could forget her decision and skip her ultimatum.

"I don't, but—"

"You don't think we should leave together. Is that it?"

"No. Not exactly." She exhaled slowly, trying to find the right words. "Actually, there is something I want to ask you."

"Anything."

She swallowed. She'd faced down tough judges, hostile witnesses and unsympathetic juries, but she'd never been as tongue-tied as now.

"What is it, Clare? It can't be that bad. I promise you I don't bite. Here, maybe I can help you relax."

"No, Anton, wait. Not until I—"

But it was too late. He had already crossed the room and had swung her chair around to work his magic on her strained shoulders and tense neck. She let him pull her up and out of her chair. She didn't complain when he pressed against the knots in her lower back. She wanted nothing more than to let him wipe away all her problems with several simple strokes of his large, gentle hands.

But she couldn't. Not yet.

He stopped, his hands dropping to his sides. She stood there for a few moments, trying to pull herself together. She turned to face him, to talk to him. Instead, she was lost in his deep blue eyes. She couldn't get the words out. She couldn't think what words to use.

"So, are you thinking the same thing I am?" he asked.

He was so close, she could feel his breath against her cheeks. She didn't move away. "I doubt it."

"I don't," he answered.

"I'm not sure this is a good idea," she whispered practically into his lips. She wanted him to tilt his head slightly forward, just a little bit so that the rest would be taken out of her hands. But he didn't move. He looked and he waited and he smiled. She shifted.

In an instant, the distance between them closed, and she was breathing him in, smelling him, tasting him. She could feel her mouth swell under his touch, her lips softening, blooming, ripening. She could feel his tongue exploring, probing for entry. She wanted to open her mouth to his, to forget about the office gossips, the Van Belden account, all that and more. She wanted to know only this.

She wanted this so much, but she couldn't do it. Not until she knew the truth.

Her lips stopped moving under his. Her hands pushed against his chest. He let her go, and she drew back.

"God, Clare!" he said between deep breaths. "Do you know what you're doing to me?"

She shuddered. She rubbed her hands up and down her arms. "I'm sorry. I can't do this."

"Why? You want me as much as I want you." He touched her cheek lightly with his knuckles.

She didn't speak, but she didn't pull back, either.

"No one has to know. You know you can trust me," he said.

She reacted as if he had slapped her, moving away and crossing the room. "Well, maybe I'm not so sure I do." She leaned against the table where they had discussed so many cases together. Exhaling slowly, she straightened her blouse. "Besides, it's too late."

"Too late? What are you talking about?"

"Everyone is already talking about us."

He narrowed his eyes. "And what exactly are they saying?"

"Oh, the usual," she said, trying to sound casual. "You know, that someone is using someone by sleeping his way up to the top."

It was his turn to react as if he had been slapped. If it was an act, it was a damn good one. "Is that what you think? Is that why you think I'm here, Clare? Why I've been— You really think I— You—" He shook his head, apparently unable to go on.

"It really never occurred to you that I might help you along if you seduced me?" Clare said, breaking the long moment of silence.

He opened his mouth to speak, but shut it firmly to glare at her instead.

"No, it didn't," he finally said. A muscle twitched in his jaw, but his voice was surprisingly calm. "If anything, I trust you to do what's best for the client, the way you always do."

He shook his head slowly, then snapped it up to glare at her again. "And if you really think otherwise, then you underestimate both of us."

Clare thought about what he said and about the man he was: the boy who had protected his mother, the adult who had joined the force and the firm so he could help other women, the colleague who hadn't mentioned seeing her drunk, the friend who had helped her relax.

Clare was almost convinced, but she had to know for sure. "So you aren't using me as a ticket to the top?"

"I just said I wasn't. What else do you want me to say? What else can I say?"

She stuck out her chin. "Prove it, Anton."

"What? How?"

"Withdraw your candidacy. Tell Brooks and Bailey that you're not interested in the account."

He opened his mouth, then closed it immediately. He stared at her for a moment. He made a strangled sound and shook his head. "I'm sorry, Clare, I can't do that. That's something I just can't do."

Lauren glanced around the room, taking in the fashion-conscious socialites making their regal appearance at the charity function. She smiled at one or two familiar faces and nodded at other acquaintances. Her preshow jitters were beginning to fade.

Lauren had frequently attended this kind of social gathering with Charles. It had been important for his business. Today she was here for Helen.

Or rather, Helen was here for her. Lauren had tried to get out of the Heart-to-Heart Benefit, but Sherelle had made it clear that her absence would not be appreciated. It was a major PR event for the newspaper, and everyone was expected to attend. So despite her growing reservations, Lauren found herself asking the younger woman to help her once again. Helen—bless her heart—had agreed immediately, making Lauren feel even guiltier. She was nothing more than a cold-hearted manipulator who used people when it suited her. She was no better than Charles, who had done that to her throughout their marriage.

But unlike Charles, Lauren was aware of other people's needs and feelings. She glanced at her watch. By this time, Frank and Alice would be having their own little heart-to-heart. That is, if Frank was as serious as he claimed.

Lauren looked around the room for Clare. She wasn't here yet. Maybe she had decided not to come. Clare had been planning to ask Anton Muller to be her escort, but maybe they'd opted for something more fun and private than a charity benefit. Good for them! Lauren was glad she'd encouraged her friend to follow her heart. Clare might present a tough and hard image, but she had a soft, vulnerable side. She could do with somebody taking care of her for a change.

And then there was Helen and Joe. Lauren hadn't been able to fix that yet, but she hoped things would look up for the two of them too, by the end of the night.

Her eyes scanned the room again, stopping on a tall, dark-haired man in deep conversation with Helen. It didn't take much to guess it was Joe. If his appearances hadn't clued her, Helen's awkwardness would have. Dressed in a short skirt and low-cut top, Helen was lovely and stylish. Yet she couldn't quite eliminate every trace of her computer geek persona. A techno geek whom Lauren had thrown to the beautiful people with all the heartlessness of the Roman emperors. Make that beautiful person, because it was Joe's proximity that was so clearly making Helen nervous.

Lauren continued to watch the two young people from a distance, observing how Joe leaned toward Helen as he talked and how she tilted her head to listen. The way his hand touched hers, the way her face glowed told Lauren they liked each other, and she didn't have to be a singles columnist to know that. Joe's disappointed look when someone invaded their intimate space was blatantly obvious. Lauren watched as Helen gave Joe an apologetic shrug and turned to address the intruder.

If Lauren was going to play Cupid, now was the time. Grabbing two glasses of wine from a passing waiter, she approached Joe. She pushed one glass in his hand.

"Drink up," she said, in the consoling voice she used with her own children.

Joe didn't take the drink. "Do I know you? Have we met?"

"Would you believe me if I said I am your fairy godmother? No? I didn't think so." She had a sip of wine and eyed him over the rim of her glass. "I'm a friend of Lauren's."

"Of Lauren's?" He reached for the glass he had just rejected. "You're not her mother, are you?"

"No, but I could be. She lives in my house. I'm Lauren, by the way," she said without thinking.

He gave her an incredulous look. "You're Lauren?"

"Yes, we're, um, both Lauren. Strange coincidence, isn't it?" She laughed lightly to cover her embarrassment.

"It certainly is. You live in the same house, you have the same name. How do people tell you apart?"

"There is the age factor."

"There is that."

"And we don't look alike."

"No, you don't."

"And we're never in the same place at the same time. Except for tonight, of course."

"Of course."

Lauren didn't miss Helen's attempt to extricate herself from the conversation she was in to join them. She caught the look of appeal that Helen cast at Joe. Either he didn't see it, or he wasn't planning on responding. That left only her.

"Oh my goodness! I have to tell Hel—Lauren something."

She pushed her way toward Helen. Maybe Helen didn't notice her edging closer. Or maybe somebody was closing in on Helen, and she just had to turn and step back. She made that swivel, stepped back and collided straight into Lauren's chest and face. Lauren's hand went up to block the collision and her wine-filled glass rose, too. When her hand came down again, the glass was empty. Helen's blond hair was dripping red liquid and her blouse was revealing more than the designer had ever intended.

"I'm so sorry. I'm so very sorry," Lauren wailed, ignoring the people who were staring at them. Her arms flailed wildly. "I… You… And then I… And you…"

"What am I going to do?" Helen asked Lauren. She ran her fingers through her hair, dripping more wine onto her blouse. "I can't stay here."

"No," Lauren agreed. She turned to Joe hovering at their elbows, a concerned look on his face.

"Joe, you take her."

"But—"

"Really, it's the only thing."

"I agree." Joe stepped to Helen's side and took her arm. "I'll take you home."

Helen hesitated for a second. Another drop of wine fell on her face and ran down her cheeks. "Okay," she said, and let Joe lead her across the room.

Lauren turned away from Joe and Helen. Where they went from here was their business. She only hoped they had a lot of fun and no regrets.

Unlike her. She had plenty of regrets.

"Somehow I didn't imagine you would be here."

"Michael!" Lauren turned to Michael Connolly, who took the empty glass from her hand, replacing it with another. "I could say the same about you."

"I always come. It's a tradition I began when I was the science writer for the paper."

"I didn't know you wrote for the paper."

"It was a long time ago, between being a publicist for your husband's firm and before I became a book author."

"You're certainly an experienced writer. I've just been a housewife."

"Just a housewife?"

"Well, I did teach for a while. Before the children."

"Teach? You never wrote a column?"

"A column? I did write some articles about the Painted Ladies movement, but hardly a column."

"Well, see, I was wondering about that the other day, when I was reading the *Gazette*. One of the columns mentioned an incident that was very familiar. Oddly so."

"Oh?"

Lauren cursed herself for writing about their date. But after Sherelle had nixed a couple of her ideas, she had been uninspired, and there simply hadn't been enough time to research singles on holiday or the single life in Chicago's many different ethnic communities.

"Yes," he went on, his eyes fixed on hers. "A woman on a blind date meets one of her ex's colleagues which leads to a quandary—should she or shouldn't she agree to a second date. Could be a version of our story."

"Could be," she agreed with a shrug. "But it's hardly unusual. It's probably just a coincidence."

"Just a coincidence?"

Something about his tone forced her to confess. "Okay, it's more." She gave him what she hoped was a self-assured grin. "I know the columnist. I told her what happened, she decided to use it. Does that annoy you?"

"It should," he said. "But it doesn't. I guess I would have done the same thing."

"Now, that I doubt." She turned to leave, but he caught hold of her wrist.

"You're not being straight with me are you, Lauren. There's more to this story, isn't there?"

He released her, and she met his gaze. Doing her best to sound like Chrissie in her rebellious-teenager tone, she said, "Like what?"

"Oh, like the fact that you wrote about that incident because you are the columnist."

"No. That would be the other Lauren." This Lauren laughed nervously, nodding in the direction of the now-departing couple. "The young woman heading toward the door. I'm a bit too old to write that column."

"In some people's eyes maybe."

"In the eyes of those who matter."

"Look, I recognize the style. I looked up your maiden name. You might as well confess, it's you."

Lauren considered the situation for a minute. What the heck? He had outed her.

"Okay, you're right. It's me. What are you going to do about it?"

* * *

Lauren wrapped herself in her old dressing gown and headed downstairs to the kitchen. She felt rested. All things considered, the evening had gone remarkably well; no big blunders on her part, no awkward moments of silence, no dreaded public revelations.

Michael had uncovered her deception, but after she had confessed, he had made it clear he wasn't going to do anything about it. He even thought it quite funny, and right now, so did she. She was on top of her world and things were finally looking pretty good.

Lauren filled the electric kettle, needing all her strength to open the tap. Someone must have hurt her fingers turning it off. But at least, her guests were getting more responsible about dealing with the ancient plumbing.

She glanced around the kitchen for any telltale signs, but there weren't any. No one else was up yet. Or maybe she was the only one around. Neither Alice nor Helen had been here when she came home last night, which she had taken as a good sign. Alice and Frank had probably had their little talk and were up to better things. As for Helen, Lauren was pretty sure she hadn't returned during the night. Even though her insomnia was gone, she remained a light sleeper and would have heard the young woman come in. Lauren hoped Helen had found someplace to stay where she did more than just sleep.

That left only Lauren in the house, with a whistling kettle. She poured hot water over a tea bag and went to the breakfast room. There was a note on the table scribbled in handwriting she recognized. She picked it up, hoping to read how Alice was making other plans for the upcoming Day in Our Village. They had talked about going together, but Lauren suspected her friend would much rather attend the annual Oak Park Festival with her husband.

She read rapidly, a smile on her face. Her expression didn't change when she placed the note back on the table. She warmed her hands around the teacup.

After she finished her tea, she walked back to the kitchen. She ran the tap again and then tried to turn it off. There was something wrong, probably a worn washer. She'd learned how to fix those, along with other minor plumbing problems when she had renovated her house.

But a strange hissing sound coming from the pipes made her take another look. There was a leak, one that a new washer could not fix. She was going to have to call a plumber.

Even without an estimate, Lauren knew any major repairs would be prohibitively expensive. With an old house like this, a plumber would most likely have to strip everything and then replace the piping. With her current financial condition, copper was completely out of the question. There was no way she could afford it, not even with the money from the column. It was already spent—had been before the first column had gone to press.

There was no two ways about it. She was going to have to sell the house. She was going to have to abandon the only thing that had kept her going since the divorce.

Lauren leaned against the wall for support. She had known it all along. Ever since the divorce, she had been on a crash course to disaster. A couple of good turns on the way hadn't changed a thing.

She reached for the phone, but didn't pick up the receiver. There was time enough to call the plumber and the real estate agent, time enough to tell Clare, Helen, Chrissie and Alice. First, she was going to have a good cry. Fortunately, there was no one around to see her.

CHAPTER 14

Something was tickling Helen's nose, making her want to sneeze. She rolled her head away, only to knock it painfully against something hard. She opened her eyes. Sunlight coming through the window almost blinded her. She tried to remember where she was. Not in her old apartment, not in Chrissie's old room in Lauren's house, but in a bigger, wider bed. My God, someone was lying next to her.

Joe.

It took Helen only a moment to remember how she had managed to wake up, naked, with a very sexy man sleeping next to her, looking completely wiped out, practically comatose. It didn't surprise her, considering how energetic he had been during the night. The perfect lover, willing to go the extra mile, to give her pleasure first—nothing at all like the few men she had known intimately before, men who didn't seem to think that a woman's response mattered in the first place.

Helen shifted to bring Joe closer into her line of vision. A wave of tenderness engulfed her as she gazed at his hair, brows, cheeks, nose, lips and chin—every piece of him perfect.

She studied each perfect feature on his face, cataloging them again, in awe that she was waking up like this, in wonder that he had wanted her here, in amazement of how good it had been—and just a little bit in doubt about the wisdom of what they had done.

There hadn't been much room for doubt last night, not once they had started to kiss. They had begun almost as soon as they got in his car. She hadn't even had time to think about how she must look and smell. The spilled wine certainly hadn't bothered Joe. He didn't stop running his fingers through her hair, kissing her wine-stained cheeks and then her wine-soaked breasts.

Yes, once the kissing had begun, any doubt had gone out the window like a screensaver at the click of a mouse. By the time they got to his place, she was too much under his influence to reason at all. It was only much later, when they lay together, her body curled against his, that she began to wonder if she'd done the right thing.

She squinted her eyes and tried to read the clock on the dresser. She had promised herself she would stay only a short while after their lovemaking. She had savored the feeling of his chest against her back, his legs tucked under hers, his arm draped around her waist, his hand cupping her breast. He'd placed it there, when she had snuggled up to him. It had grown heavy and then dropped, as his breathing deepened, his exhalations tickling her nape.

She had closed her eyes, knowing it would be better to leave than to face the morning after. But she hadn't been able to get up. One more minute, she had told herself. Just one more.

She must have fallen asleep, and now here she was, the sunlight pouring through the window. She didn't want to wake Joe. She didn't want him sitting up and forcing her to stay. Not that it would take much forcing.

She really had to go, to get away before she blurted out the truth about masquerading as Lauren, about her real feelings for him. She had come very close to doing that last night.

Helen freed herself from under Joe's hold and wriggled into her rumpled clothes. She picked up her shoes, planning to put them on when she'd shut the door behind her. She had to get away from this temptation. She couldn't betray Lauren, not even for Joe, not when it was thanks to Lauren that Helen was here in the first place. Besides, she had promised to do this for Lauren, and a promise is a promise.

Helen knew what she had to do. She didn't have to discuss it with Chrissie. They had shared so much in the past, but this would have to remain Helen's secret. Chrissie would not be forced to choose between her mother and her friend.

Anyway, soon it would be all over. Helen would

return to who she was meant to be: a computer geek, consigned to her programs and hard drives the way Cinderella was exiled to her ashes. There would be no Cinderella-ending for her because only fairy-tale princesses get their handsome princes. Helen wasn't a princess, she was a geek. And even if she weren't, there was no way Joe would come looking for her—glass slipper or high-heeled sandal in hand—once he learned what she had done.

On Monday, Lauren decided to consult with someone about her decision to sell the house.

Helen hadn't been around much over the weekend. She had mumbled something about having work to finish at the university. Lauren suspected Helen didn't want to admit to spending time with Joe, but she discovered this was not the case when Joe called looking for Helen. Lauren couldn't help him and she didn't think she should. Helen must have her own reasons for keeping out of his way. In the meantime, Lauren had time enough to tell Helen about the house, to let her know they were abandoning the masquerade.

Because after hearing the plumber's estimate and mulling the issue for two days, Lauren was certain that selling the house was her only option. She even looked up the number of a real estate agent, someone she had met through Charles.

Yet, she hesitated. Should she talk it out with her

friends first? She hadn't heard from Alice since Friday night when Lauren had left her to go to the Heart-to-Heart. She was obviously working through her own domestic issues, and Lauren just couldn't pull her away from that.

Lauren tried phoning Chrissie, but kept getting the answering machine. This wasn't the kind of topic to discuss through e-mail.

That left Clare, who as a lawyer was sure to know all the details about taxes and closing costs and would probably provide the best advice. But she, too, seemed to have disappeared. Anne, Clare's assistant, claimed she was out of town.

Left alone with her dark thoughts, Lauren went ahead on her own and dialed the number of the real estate agent.

When the phone rang later that afternoon, Lauren was still upset about her decision. She had spent most of the morning moping. But the die was cast, and if the real estate agent was as good as her reputation, things were going to move very fast.

Certain that the agent was calling about the house, she picked up the receiver.

"Lauren?"

"Speaking."

"It's Charles. Don't tell me you don't recognize my voice?"

Truth be told, she hadn't. Surely that was a good sign, the first since Saturday.

"I guess I wasn't expecting to hear from you. How are you, Charles?"

Did she really want to know? She had her own life to worry about.

"Things are going well," he said. "Andrew Olsen is retiring next year, and there's a good chance I will be named president."

"I'm happy to hear that, Charles. I'm happy for you."

But, of course, she wasn't. How could she be when her own life was taking more hits than a pileup on the freeway? How could she when she was about to sign away the only asset she had salvaged from their divorce?

"Did you have anything specific to tell me, or were you hoping we would celebrate by phone?" Would he catch the sarcasm in her voice? Probably not.

"You wouldn't believe me, would you, if I said I just wanted to see how you are?"

Belief in his feelings for her was something she had lost a long time ago. Instead of reassuring him, she breathed loudly into the receiver so he could know her annoyance. "Well, now that we've got that out of the way, maybe you can tell me what's really going on. I've got a lot to do today. I really don't have time for conversations."

Charles sighed, but he dropped the chitchat and got to the point. "I hear you're putting the house up for sale."

"News gets around."

And how quickly! He must have been sitting in the agent's office when she called. Or perhaps he had been waiting for this all along, even set it up. No. She refused to consider that possibility. Charles may be a lout in many ways, but he wouldn't deliberately sabotage her. Would he?

"I guess we have the same real estate agent," he said. "She knew we… I was looking for something and called me."

Lauren noted the blunder and her suspicions grew. He *was* calling about the house. He was after it.

But why? It was her family house, and he had never shared her love for it, never been interested in its history or cared about its restoration. During their divorce proceedings, he had relinquished it to her without a single objection.

"I know you must be pretty desperate if you're selling it, and I'd like to help you out, if I can."

He cleared his throat. She could picture him tugging on his tie, the way he did when he was uneasy. The way he did when he was trying to wing it through a lie. She'd seen and heard the gesture often enough to recognize it.

"I'd like to buy it," he said.

"Buy the house?"

She knew it. She knew it! He wanted her house. Or maybe Tracie did. It didn't matter. They wanted the house. They wanted *her* house.

"Yes, buy the house," he said. "At the market price, of course."

Of course. So much for wanting to help her! It sounded more like he wanted to help himself with the best deal. He knew the house was worth considerably more than its market price, and as usual, he had his own best interests at heart. He didn't want her house at all. He just wanted a good deal, and he probably thought she was desperate enough to sell it.

But he didn't really know her, and he certainly didn't know the woman she had become. She wasn't going to let him get away with it. She may be down, but she wasn't defeated. She may be single, but she had lots of friends—and she had a few tricks up her sleeve. She wouldn't sell him the house. Never!

"I'll think about it, Charles," she said. "I'll discuss it with the agent and with my lawyer, and I'll let you know."

"Don't take too long, Lauren," he said. "Tracie's condo is getting too small for us, and we'd like to move out soon. There are other houses in the neighborhood."

"Like I said, Charles, I'll think about it, and let you know."

"Who can tell me how we go from here to here?"

Professor Wartowski pointed to two equations and glanced around the small group of graduate students. Helen kept her face down. The only problem she could focus on was her situation with Joe. There was that other equation also, the one with Lauren in there, somewhere.

But it wasn't Lauren's fault that the sum of Joe and Helen didn't add up. Joe would figure it out soon enough. He'd stop calling, stop leaving messages for Lauren to leave on Helen's bedroom door. It was Lauren the columnist he liked, not Helen the brain. Helen didn't need to be able to do Professor Wartowski's problems to know that.

She blinked at the scribbling covering the paper in front of her. Joe's face stared back at her, like a figure emerging from a maze of half-connected dot-to-dots. It was a beautiful face. But now she was remembering the admiring glance he'd given her when she had helped him with his Web pages, the gentle concern he'd expressed for her wine-drenched hair, the eyes clouded with a desire for her.

Maybe he could forgive her after all.

Helen lifted her head. A classmate was pointing to a number and saying something. She squinted at the equation reflected on the wall. That square root didn't belong there. And the variable…

"No," she heard herself protesting. "The z variable shouldn't be factored in at that point."

In a single movement, everyone in the class turned toward her.

Professor Wartowski beamed at her. "Thank you,

Helen. I knew I could count on you. Would you like to take over?"

"Um, um, sure."

She walked forward without a thought to the clip-clopping of her high heels. She liked math. She was good at programming. If Joe couldn't deal with that, she had no place with him.

There was only one way to find out. Tell him. Surely Lauren could understand that.

If Charles thought Lauren would spend all her time thinking about him and his generous offer, he was wrong. She had a column to write and letters to answer. Feeling better than she had in days, she turned on her computer. She browsed through her in-box, bypassing the addresses she didn't recognize to take more time with the ones she did. The new mail that Sherelle had forwarded really grabbed her attention.

To: lauren@onsurf.com
From: sherelle@chicgazette.com
Subject: *leslie hour*
hey lauren, good to see u on friday but sorry u had to leave wet and dripping. wanted to tell u: the *leslie hour* is doing a special on the singles scene and would like you to be their main guest. you can't say no. great publicity for your column, great things sure to follow! let's talk. forget talk. let's par-tay!—s

* * *

Lauren thought her heart was going to give out. She was too old to take this kind of shock, too worn-out to continue on this roller coaster of disastrous news and heaven-sent follow-up.

Because there was no doubt that this was the kind of lucky break she had never expected. Appearing on a morning television chat show wouldn't pay her plumbing bill, but, as Sherelle mentioned, the *Leslie Hour* was her ticket to more contracts, more money. It was the break that could lead to keeping the house in her hands and out of Charles's.

She just had to say yes, and she just had to make sure Helen would, too.

Lauren knew she had to act soon. The show was to be filmed live in two days time. Enough time to rehearse their appearance, enough time for cold feet. Lauren was pretty sure hers would remain very warm, even hot for the duration, especially considering the rewards and alternatives. Helen was the weak link in the chain, and Lauren was not going to let her break it.

With the single-mindedness she had recently discovered, she prepared her strategy. With a ruthlessness she didn't know she had, she planned her attack. She didn't even discuss it with her friends and especially not with her daughter. Chrissie and Helen were best friends, after all, and although Chrissie had been sure that Helen wouldn't mind when it came to lending her face, television changed everything. Lauren really didn't want her daughter to try to talk her out of it.

When Helen arrived that evening, Lauren was ready. She waited until they were eating the special dinner she'd prepared, hoping the way to a woman's will was the same as to a man's heart.

"I have some really good news to share with you," she said with a smile. So this is what the Wicked Stepmother felt when she offered Snow White the poisoned apple.

"About Alice?"

Lauren nearly lost her smile. She still didn't know how her best friend was doing. She would call her tomorrow, first thing. But now, she just had to get on with this.

"No, not about Alice. About me. About us."

"Us? You mean the column? I was going to ask you about that. You see, I've been thinking, and I—"

Lauren didn't wait for Helen to continue. "Looks like we're finally going to resolve this."

"You told them, Lauren? We don't have to continue to pretend anymore. That's great! That's so totally great!"

Helen's face brightened and her voice filled with enthusiasm. Lauren told herself that she wasn't going to ruin everything. She really wasn't. She was going to fix everything soon—very, very soon. Just not yet.

"Actually, I didn't tell them about it."

"Oh." Helen's face fell. She looked down at her

plate. She didn't prompt Lauren for any more information, but she smiled sadly.

Lauren had to hand it to Helen: she was being a sport, a real sport. Unlike herself who would probably get a lifetime membership to the Self-Serving Scumballs of the Universe Society. She would be right there at the top of the list, ahead of Charles, ahead of the Wicked Stepmother.

"I didn't get the chance to tell Sherelle." That, at least, was true. "Because she had something to tell me first. The column's been such a success, we've been invited to appear on the *Leslie Hour*."

"That's good, Lauren," Helen said, toying with her food.

"Yes, it is. And it's all thanks to you."

"To me?" Helen's head lifted.

Pleased with the eye contact, Lauren nodded. "Yes, thanks to you. I would never have pulled it off without you. You made a great impression on everybody Friday night."

"But I didn't do anything. I wasn't there long enough. I left early. You know, with…" Helen looked down at her food again.

"Apparently, you made enough of an impression that they want you on television."

"Me on television? Television! Lauren, I can't go on television."

"Of course you can. You'll be fine."

Helen shook her head vigorously. "No, Lauren, you don't understand, I can't go on television."

"Of course you can."

"No, I can't."

"Why not?"

"Because I'm not Lauren Wilt. You are. I'd never pull it off."

"I don't see why not. You're a beautiful, intelligent and articulate woman. You'll dazzle everyone. No one would have a problem believing you are Lauren Wilt, a journalist."

"The people who know me would. It's one thing to show up at the newspaper. It's another thing to go in front of a national audience."

"You may have a point." A concession here could earn Lauren more points elsewhere. "But I think you underestimate yourself. Everyone who knows you would probably be surprised they didn't see your potential earlier."

Lauren was intent on persuading Helen. But she sincerely meant what she'd just said. It wasn't just the change of clothes (right now Helen was wearing her faded jeans and an oversized T-shirt). Nor was it her demeanor: Helen was still a shy computer geek, but her intelligence shone through.

"I think you can do it, Helen," Lauren repeated. "I think you'll be fine."

"Oh, I don't know."

"We'll work on it. We'll get ready for it. I'll coach you. You'll be fine. You'll see."

"No. I can't do it, Lauren. I know I said I'd help. I really want to, but I can't do this. I can't go on television. Not for you, Lauren, not even for you."

Faced with Helen's reluctance, Lauren decided to play her last card. The pity card.

"I need the money, Helen. Without it, I'm going to have to sell the house."

"What?"

Lauren explained about the leak and the estimate and the real estate agent, but she didn't go into Charles's phone call. It might have been the straw that had broken *her* back, but mentioning it to Helen would be too low a blow. When she finished, she folded her hands in front of her and waited for Helen to make the next move.

"Okay, Lauren, I'll do it. But—"

Lauren raised her right hand up, as if she were being sworn in. "Absolutely. It's the last thing I'll ask of you."

"Actually, what I wanted to say was that I'll do it on one condition."

"Name it."

"I tell Joe the truth first."

Three days ago, Lauren would have agreed. But now, she couldn't, not with everything else at stake.

"You can't do that, Helen. He works for Sherelle. He won't be able to keep it from her."

"But I, he…" Helen gave her a funny look. "He has to know. I have to tell him. He'll never forgive me."

She looked away from Lauren, her voice fading to a whisper. Lauren watched her for a moment and considered her best shot. But Helen looked so miserable and so unhappy, that all thought of strategy and attack and Charles went out the window. To hell with it, other things were far more important.

"Are you in love with him?"

"I don't know, maybe, I think so. This has never happened to me before, Lauren." Helen lifted her hands up in the air, and then dropped them to her sides.

Lauren wanted to call off the whole thing. More than that, she wanted to assure Helen that she could have any man she wanted, including Joe. She wanted to give her a page out of her own book and tell her that who she was didn't depend on the man she chose and the husband who abandoned her. Life didn't stop because one dream came to an end. There were a million others to try. But those were lessons Helen had to learn on her own.

"Do this for me, and I'll talk to him. I'll make it right for you. You'll see. After tomorrow, I'll make everything right again."

Lauren didn't know how she would do it, but she knew somehow she would.

CHAPTER 15

"You look fine," Lauren said to Helen who was still fussing over her clothes, even as she was being pushed out the door. "Besides, I'm sure there'll be a professional makeup artist on the set to make sure you look great. Just get in the car and go."

"You'll be there?"

"Right behind you. Just remember, breathe deep, stay calm. It'll be over before you know it. Now go. And, Helen…" Lauren waited for the young woman to look her in the eye, then said, "Thanks a lot. Really."

Helen nodded and headed out the door. She had to be at the studio early, so they had decided to go separately. Besides, before Lauren went, she had to talk to Clare about whether there was something illegal in this public deception. Because it was one thing to fool the paper, it was something else to do it on television. She didn't want Helen to pay the price. She was already being so understanding about Joe.

But Clare was out of town. Or rather, as her personal assistant hinted, out of reach. She was holed up at home for some reason. So it was to Clare's home that Lauren went.

Lauren rang the bell and pounded on the door repeatedly before Clare relented and appeared.

She looked as if she had a very bad bout of flu. Her eyes were runny and bloodshot, her cheeks puffy and pale, her nose red and swollen.

Lauren's heart went out to the formidable woman, who, for once, displayed vulnerability.

"You look awful, Clare. You should have called. You know I would have come."

But Lauren wondered whether she would have. She was sending Helen to the wolves, and she was about to grill Clare, when she was obviously sick, about a complicated legal question. Lauren was allowing her obsession with her house to ruin everything. It couldn't be worth it.

But she wouldn't let herself think about it. "Mind if I come in for a minute?"

"It's not contagious, if that's what you're asking." Clare stepped back to let Lauren enter. "It's not that bad, actually. I look worse than I feel."

"But bad enough not to go to work?"

"Work is... Let's just say, work is a bit difficult to deal with these days."

"Difficult? That's never been a problem for you." Lauren stepped closer to her friend. Clare's head was bent, but Lauren could have sworn there were tears in her dark eyes. "Hey, what's wrong, Clare?"

"Oh, Lauren. I've been such a fool!"

Right there and then, a sobbing Clare fell into Lauren's arms. Without looking at her watch, Lauren knew the minutes were ticking by. The filming would begin in an hour, and Helen needed her. Lauren hoped she wouldn't have to choose between her friends, but she couldn't turn down this appeal for comfort from a woman who she would have sworn never, ever cried. She patted Clare's back gently, urging her as best as she could to let it all out. When the sobbing stopped, Lauren suggested they share a pot of tea.

"Do you want to tell me what this is about?"

"No… I… It's…"

Lauren didn't have to look at Clare, seated at the kitchen island, to know she was still crying. "Sometimes it helps to talk."

Clare sniffled, but shook her head.

"I am a good listener." Lauren worked her way around the island and prepared everything for tea.

Clare didn't say anything. She just sat there. Lauren wondered if she would be able to hold her mug. She pushed it closer, resisting the urge to lift it to Clare's lips, the way she used to for Chrissie and Jeff.

"I know it's difficult for you to open up, but sometimes it helps."

Clare's only reaction was a sniffle and a sob, but she reached for her mug and wrapped her hands around it.

Lauren didn't know what else she could say. She

glanced at her watch. She was running out of time, and she could no longer count on gentle persuasion.

"Look, Clare, right now, I'm on the verge of losing my house. If it weren't for Helen, it would be a sure thing. I want to help you, but I need to be with her. So unless you start talking, I'm going to have to leave. Now, for the last time, talk to me. Tell me what's going on."

Clare looked at Lauren as if she were speaking Chinese. Then, as if she were coming out of a trance, she straightened in her chair. Her eyes lost their dazed look.

"It's about Anton."

"Yes? You were going to invite him to the Heart-to-Heart." Lauren had been so immersed in her problems, she'd forgotten to ask Clare how that had turned out. Obviously not too well, given the way she looked.

"No. I didn't invite him. I couldn't... I didn't... I knew, I just knew I shouldn't get close to a colleague. But he..." Clare turned her face away. "Oh, Lauren! I've been such a stupid idiot."

Her eye on her watch and the minutes ticking by, Lauren patted Clare gently on the back and waited. Bit by bit, the story emerged.

"So let me get this straight." Lauren was finally able to recap. "You gave him an ultimatum, you or the account, and he said no?"

"Yes. He said no, he wouldn't give up the account."

"And that was it for you? You asked him to get out of your life?"

"Yes, of course. He was using me."

"Oh, Clare."

"Go ahead, say it. It can hardly be any worse than what I've been saying to myself. I've been such a stupid, blind idiot."

Lauren shook her head. "No, no, no. Nothing like that. On the contrary. You just don't know how to trust."

"I trusted him. He betrayed me."

"I don't think so."

"How can you say that? He admitted it. He was only interested in me because he wants that account, and he thinks I'm so stupid and naive and besotted, I'll give it to him."

"Oh, Clare. I don't think he thinks that at all. Just imagine how he must feel."

"Sorry that I found out."

"Angry because you don't trust him. Think how you would feel if a man accused you of coming on to him only because of the job he could give you."

Clare glared at her. "It's not like that."

"Of course, it is. You're telling him you don't trust him."

"I do trust him. I mean, I did, but I don't." Her hands dropped into her lap. "Oh, I don't know."

Forgetting the time, Lauren continued, "No, you don't trust him. You don't even trust yourself when it comes to him. This isn't about Anton, is it? It's about you."

When Clare didn't respond, Lauren went on. "Look,

I know how important your career is to you, how much it matters, how you've been misled and hurt in the past, but you were very young then, and it was another man. You can't keep punishing yourself like this."

Clare kept her eyes on the mug in front of her. The minutes ticked by as the silence stretched between them. Lauren wanted to shake her friend into responding, but instead she spoke softly, putting together the whole picture from the few details that Clare had revealed over the years.

"You've dedicated your whole life to your career, believing it can shield you from heartache. Well maybe it can sometimes, but even the most solid crutch can't protect you from everything. That's when it's no longer a crutch, it's an impediment."

"An impediment?" Clare lifted her head and made a sound between a laugh and a huff. "Lauren, this is not some column full of clichés that you can spin. This is about me."

"But I am talking about you. Your career has become an impediment to trusting yourself and taking a risk. Forget about principles, reputations and scandals. Think of all you can have with Anton. Go ahead, Clare, take a risk."

At that moment, Lauren realized she was no longer talking just about Clare. "I can't believe I'm telling you this. You've been saying the same thing to me all along."

"I have?"

"You told me to sell the house and make a big break, and when I wouldn't, you called me a coward. When I couldn't meet my bills and taxes, you told me I was using the house as a crutch, that I was tied to one way of life. Remember? Well, that's exactly what you're doing."

"My work is not my crutch. It's my life," Clare said.

"My point exactly. Some kind of life, if it doesn't let you live."

Lauren looked at her watch, suddenly remembering where she should be. "I'd love to stay and explain it to you. I'd love to convince you that you should take the risk, but if I don't leave right now I'm going to make the biggest mistake in my adult life. So why don't you get dressed and come with me?"

For the first time in her life, Lauren wished she had sirens in her car. She had to get to the studio on time. She had to get there for Helen.

"Hey, careful!" Clare said from the passenger seat. "You just drove through another red light."

"Sorry." Lauren didn't ease her foot off the gas.

"Do that again, and I'll make you pull over! I only let you drive because I thought I was upset. But I think I'm less dangerous behind the wheel than you."

"I'm not upset. I just need to get to the studio on time."

"You have to get to the studio on time." Clare imitated Lauren's voice. Then she continued in her own voice. "Are you going to tell me what this is about?"

"Well, it's like this…" Lauren began, and somehow she managed to keep an eye on the traffic, while telling Clare everything that had happened since Friday night, including Charles's offer on her house.

"God, Lauren. What a saga!"

Lauren smiled at her friend. The Eisenhower Expressway was unusually empty. If the other roads were as traffic free, they had nothing to worry about.

Clare looked out the window for a moment, then back at Lauren. "I'm sorry I did a vanishing act. I'm sorry I wasn't there for you. My life was crashing and I just didn't know what to do."

"And now?"

"I still don't." She braced a hand on the dashboard. "Do you really think I'm afraid to trust myself?"

"I think we all are. That's what I've just realized. All of us—you, me, Helen—all this time, we've been holding on to things, hoping they would protect us. Me with my house, you with your career, Helen with her clothes and dating manuals. Even Alice with her marriage."

"Alice took a risk. She walked out."

"Yes, she did. And think how much guts that took. She loves Frank."

"But she risked losing him because she couldn't let just the habit of her twenty-five-year marriage hold them together. I hope it paid off."

Lauren glanced at Clare. "It did."

"She's gone back to him?"

"He begged her to come back. Promised her the stars, the moon, everything, anything."

"You're kidding?"

Lauren grinned. "About the stars and the moon, yes. But he will sell the television, if she wants him to. And he's even agreed to go to counseling, if necessary. Which is probably the most you can hope from a guy anyway."

Lauren didn't mention her role in what had to have been a tearful reunion. It didn't matter because Alice and Frank had done the real work.

"Well, that's good news."

"It is. But she had to take a risk."

"To trust herself and him." Clare sighed deeply. "You know something? You might be right."

"Does that mean you're going to give Anton a chance?"

"I don't know. I keep thinking of all the possible problems."

"Stop thinking and trust yourself!"

Clare laughed. "I'm sorry for what I said about your column. You should write about this. It would be a great topic."

"Maybe. I'm not sure I want to. And you're right also. I have been confusing my life with my column."

When Lauren didn't offer any more explanation, Clare continued, "So, what are *you* going to do? Are you really going to let Helen do this? There'll no walking back afterward. Not for you, not for her."

"I know."

Clare had just given her the perfect cue. This was the right moment to ask her about the legalities of their situation, but suddenly it didn't matter. Lauren's mind was contemplating much more important things, things that had less to do with legalities and more to do with friendship and trust.

She had been so bent on keeping her house that she had forgotten what really mattered. A house is not a home. Without friends and family, what would her old Victorian mean? She had forgotten the lessons learned when writing her first book. A house is not the sum of its architecture, features, embellishments or interior decoration. A house is the history of the people who live in it, the spirit they left behind. And it was the people—her friends—Lauren was ignoring in her scramble to keep her house. Would she really want it if she messed everything up for Helen? What would it mean if Alice and Clare didn't come to visit? What difference would it make if Chrissie were disappointed in her?

All because she hadn't been able to trust herself. She had wanted to keep the house because she thought it would give her what she had lost—a marriage, a family. But she had ignored and forgotten the new family of her single life. She had forgotten her friends.

Lauren pressed down on the gas and, with a quick check over her shoulders, moved to the fast lane. She just had to get to the studio on time.

* * *

There were no parking spaces at the studio.

"You go," Clare said. "I'll take care of the car."

Lauren didn't hesitate. "Thanks, Clare. Oh, and keep your fingers crossed for me, will you?"

"Sure." She lifted her hand up to show her she was doing just that.

Lauren jumped out of the car, headed up the stairs and pushed her way into the lobby of the building.

"I need to get in," she said to the teenager posing as a security guard.

"Do you have a stage pass?" he asked.

"No. But if you just—"

"I'm sorry. You'll have to leave."

"But, you don't understand—"

"Ma'am, you have to leave now. If you don't go of your own accord, I'm going to have ask someone to escort you."

Lauren dragged her fingers through her hair. She had made it with only moments to spare, and a security guard younger than her children was going to stop her? How was she going to get past him if he continued to refuse?

She saw a slight movement behind him. If Mohammed wouldn't go to the mountain, maybe the mountain would come to Mohammed. But it was neither the mountain nor Mohammed she called out to.

"Joe!" She waved her hands and jumped up and

down, ignoring the guard's efforts to push her out of the way. "Joe! Over here!"

"Lauren?" He moved toward her. "What's going on?"

"I can't explain now, but I need to get to Helen."

He looked at her, a frown on his handsome face, assessing the situation. She didn't know how she did it—but she knew she had convinced him when he nodded. He instructed the guard to let her through.

"I'll vouch for her," he said.

"Thanks, Joe." Lauren smiled at the guard as she walked past him. "Where are they filming and what's the fastest way there?"

"That would be the elevator." Joe walked her toward it and pushed the up button. "It's not here. We could try the stairs."

"Yes, the stairs."

She followed him to the service stairs, which were undergoing some servicing of their own and were not accessible.

They headed back to the elevator. The wait seemed interminable. Lauren wanted to break into a run as soon as she stepped out of the car, but she had no idea which way to head. She followed Joe who, recognizing the urgency, quickened his pace.

They entered the studio. Lauren's eyes flew immediately to the set. No one there! Joe tapped her shoulder and pointed to a group heading their way.

"Stop," Lauren said in the loud, booming voice that

had commanded over children's birthday parties and teenage sleepovers. "Stop. She can't go on."

The group continued toward the set.

Lauren stepped forward. "Stop," she repeated.

"Who the hell are you?" someone said. "Call security and get her out of here."

"No, wait!" Lauren ignored the menacing looks she was getting. She pointed at Helen. "She can't go on because she didn't write the column. She's not Lauren Wilt. I am."

For a second, everyone was silent, then they all started to talk at once. Lauren's ears were ringing from all the questions.

"Enough!" a woman standing next to Helen said. "Enough!"

The command worked. Everyone stopped like children at a game of musical statues. They looked at the woman, they looked at Lauren and they looked back at the woman and waited for further instructions.

"We don't have time for this," the woman said. "We're on live in less than ten minutes, and the show must go on."

"It can't," Lauren insisted. "Not as planned."

"Okay, start explaining."

Lauren addressed the person who would be most hurt by the revelation she was going to make.

"I'm sorry, Sherelle," she said. "I never meant it to go

this far. You were happy with the column, so I didn't think my age was an issue. Then, you asked to meet me. I panicked, and Helen agreed to pretend to be me. We lied and deceived you, but we never intended to hurt anyone."

Sherelle was shocked enough to be speechless. The woman who had spoken up earlier, took charge again. "Let me get this straight," she said. "You're saying you wrote the columns, and she pretended to be you." She pointed at Helen, who was so pale that Lauren thought she might faint.

"Yes, but we didn't mean…"

"Never mind about the apologies. You'll get your chance to apologize soon enough. As I said, the show must go on, and what a show it's going to be. That okay, Leslie?" She turned to the talk show host. "You in?"

"I'm in. Definitely in."

CHAPTER 16

Helen watched Lauren interact with the talk show host. Lauren was laughing now at something the host had said. She seemed so relaxed, almost as if she had forgotten she was speaking in front of a camera. That wasn't how it had been when Lauren had first stepped on the set. She could barely utter monosyllables. Leslie had had to do most of the talking. She had drawn answers out of Lauren, one by one, until she had got over her stage fright and spoke easily.

Helen didn't think *she* would have been able to do it. She would have had everyone wondering how a silent geek could have written those provocative columns. But it didn't matter now because all's well that ends well.

Although…there was still one big problem.

Even if Joe could forgive Helen's deception, he wasn't going to be interested in a computer geek. Because, Helen knew for sure, that's who she was. She was finished with trying to change. She wanted to go back to her algorithms and computers. Maybe one day, she'd find her prince. And if she didn't, well, there were worse things in life than being single.

Lauren was saying something about that now, about how every single was unique. Leslie and other guests were laughing. Even Sherelle was laughing. She hadn't been earlier though.

Sherelle wasn't as good at hiding her reaction. She had been silent through most of the interview. Maybe she was still trying to understand everything. Or maybe she was just trying to decide what she wanted to do about it. The good thing was that she couldn't take it out on Lauren, not now, in public. And if things worked out as they should, maybe she never would. So Lauren would get to write her column, keep her house and live happily ever after with all her friends. It was almost as good as in books.

"Is there anything you would like to say before we end?" Leslie was asking Lauren.

"Actually, yes. I would like to apologize again. I know what we did..." Lauren shook her head and smiled in Helen's direction. "What *I* did was wrong, but I didn't want to hurt anyone. I only did what most writers do. I told stories—partly fiction, mostly true—hoping that others might enjoy them, identify with them, learn from them. So maybe it's time to tell one last story."

Helen watched, fascinated, as Lauren shifted in her seat and faced the camera.

"Once, a long time ago, another writer was involved in a similar hoax. Cyrano de Bergerac was in love with a beautiful woman, but he didn't think she could ever love anyone as ugly and grotesque and old as he. He had a handsome friend, who didn't know anything about love and fine words, who was also in love with the beautiful Roxanne. So the ugly writer lent his beautiful words to the dashing but dull suitor, and together they wooed the fair maiden.

"Cyrano wrote beautiful love letters, which his friend signed. Cyrano coached his friend in the art of seduction, supplied him with romantic lines, rescued him from awkward moments. Cyrano was so good at writing and speaking, that beautiful Roxanne fell in love. Not with the handsome young officer, but with the soul she saw in his words, Cyrano's. But there was no happily ever after for this tragic love triangle."

Lauren paused and looked around the studio. She nodded at Helen. Then, she turned to the camera and continued.

"I hope that my story will end differently. Not that I love the man Helen loves. I know that younger men are in, but cradle robbing isn't." Lauren paused for the laughter to subside. "No, I hope that in my story Helen gets her man. I hope he realizes that it is Helen he likes. I hope he is not blinded by the imaginary woman who writes the letters and dresses the part, but that he is dazzled by Helen—talented, intelligent, sometimes shy, sometimes awkward Helen. But always the best friend anyone could ever have."

* * *

After parking the car, Clare arrived too late to witness exactly how Lauren resolved the situation, too late to observe everyone's reaction, but in time to see that Lauren had gone on TV live.

She hadn't expected Lauren to confess on the air. She'd thought Lauren would convince the producers to postpone the broadcast. But Lauren had spared herself no blows and, watching her now, Clare hoped she wouldn't take too many. She didn't worry about what would happen with the column. Legally, Lauren was completely protected—Clare had seen to that—and the six-month period she had signed for was almost over. Besides, given the attention tonight's broadcast was going to get them, neither the *Chicago Gazette* nor the *Leslie Show* could hold her responsible for anything. On the contrary, they would get a nice run for their money—and no hard feelings to boot. The paper might even ask Lauren to sign for another six months.

It was Lauren Gard's reputation Clare was concerned about. Who knew how readers of the serious, literary writer would react when they learned she had been posing as a saucy singles columnist? Who knew what her editor would say? Her agent? Her reviewers? Not to mention the publicity-hungry trend-followers, silent and adulating during the brief moment of glory, but cutting and poisonous when it was over. Clare would bet her latest Jimmy Choos they would spare Lauren no humiliation. She would lose all her credibility in those circles. She might never win back the respect she deserved.

Lauren could have held on to her house and her literary reputation by not going up there. But clearly, she didn't care. Inspired by a sense of honor, she was correcting a wrong. She trusted her audience to understand and to judge her work on its merit. More than that, she trusted in her ability to pull through, no small victory for a woman who, only six months ago, believed her life was over.

Clare listened to Lauren compare her and Helen's story to Cyrano's and thought about how they differed. Lauren had never actually told Helen what to do and what to say. The younger woman had figured it out all by herself. She had been terrified, but she had trusted herself to take the leap.

Maybe it was time for Clare to do the same. Maybe it was time for her to stop playing her own Cyrano, dividing herself into the unhappy lover and the committed professional. Maybe it was time for her to stop thinking like a lawyer and start reacting like a woman and believing in her heart.

"Helen?"

Helen wanted to keep walking, to break into a run. Anything to put distance between herself and that voice. But she couldn't. She owed Joe more than a cowardly flight. She turned to face him. She would get this over with. Then she could crawl back to her hole and have a good cry.

"Joe! I was looking for you," she said. It wasn't exactly a lie.

"Helen, I—"

"No," she said, with a sudden burst of courage, inspired by Lauren. "Let me go first. Let me apologize. I am sorry. I wanted to tell you, but I couldn't."

"I know."

"Because of Lauren, you see. Because she thought she would lose the column."

"I know."

"I couldn't take the risk because someone else was involved."

"I know."

"Because she…" Helen stopped, suddenly noticing the smile on Joe's face. "You know?"

"Yes."

"And you don't mind? You still want to talk to me."

"What's there to mind? You're a very loyal person, Helen. You're a good friend, a *very* good friend. Your friends are very lucky."

Helen wanted to pinch herself to make sure she wasn't hallucinating.

He laughed and looked at her tenderly. "Well, actually, I would have preferred if you had told me. I was going to ask you—"

"You suspected?"

"Well, kind of."

"And it didn't matter, you still…" She turned away, not able to continue.

He grasped her shoulders and forced her to face him. "Still what, Helen?"

She focused on her shoes and said in a very small voice, "Still wanted to make love to me."

"Of course! That's when I wanted to ask you. That night, after we, after…well, anyway. But you left, and I couldn't get in touch with you after."

"Oh Joe, I'm so sorry. I felt horrible after that because I was lying to you. And I knew that I couldn't look you in the eyes again without telling you the truth. And I couldn't tell you because I promised."

"That's the reason why you wouldn't answer my calls? Why you were avoiding me?"

She nodded.

"It's not because you…because it wasn't…good for you?"

He was avoiding her eye. He wasn't shy or embarrassed, was he? He couldn't be. Not Joe.

"Not good for me? Oh no, Joe. No. No. No. How could you think that? It was good for me. It was the best ever."

A grin began to spread across his face. "Well, that's good because I felt that way myself, and I hope we can do it again."

"Oh, Joe!" Helen said, suddenly as full of self-assurance as when she discussed algorithms. She pulled his head down to hers to show him she hoped the same thing, too. What happened then had nothing to do with numbers, variables and equations and everything to do with delicious explosions in her body and head.

"I'm so glad this is over because now you have to honor our deal," Joe said when they drew apart.

"Our deal?"

"We agreed that I wouldn't ask you out until after you stopped writing the column." He planted a kiss on her nose. "And then *you* would ask *me*."

"So that you could find out about the real me." She remembered the conversation as if it were yesterday.

"I already know a lot about the real you, enough to know that Lauren's wish will come true. It's *who* you are, not *what* you are that I like."

"Even though I'm a computer geek? Because I am, you know. And I'm not going to change. I like math and computers, and I'm very good at them. Much better than at dressing fashionably and writing a column."

"You are beautiful," Joe said, with such conviction in his voice that she believed him. "And for the record, you're not a geek, you are a whiz. I love that about you most."

It wasn't difficult to find Anton's apartment. It was much more difficult for Clare to knock on the door. She almost turned around and ran. But a vision of Lauren facing down a camera stood between her and the stairs. She lifted her hand and knocked. Anton opened it almost immediately, a towel in his hand and his hair wet.

"Clare, what the—"

"Do you mind if I come in? There's something I'd like to say."

He stepped aside, and she entered. She was too anxious to notice anything more than a cluttered tabletop, an expensive music system and chairs that looked comfortable and inviting. She turned to face him.

He tossed the towel aside and stood there, in a T-shirt, jeans and bare feet. He must have just gotten out of the shower or bed.

"I'm not interrupting something?" She looked around, alert for any telltale signs.

"No." He looked down, straightening out his shirt. "I wasn't expecting you."

"I didn't call. I was afraid you wouldn't want to see me."

On the drive over, Clare had speculated what she would say. She had rehearsed a speech, but now she realized there was only one thing she could say. "I'm sorry. I'm so sorry."

"Clare—"

"I'm sorry I tried to push you into making a choice."

"Clare, you don't—"

"I'm sorry I tried to interfere in your professional life."

"Clare, I don't think you—"

She held up her hand, insisting he wait. "Most of all, I'm sorry I didn't trust you enough to believe you cared about me, not about your advancement in the firm."

"Clare, you don't have to do this. You don't have to apologize. I was also out of line. I want to explain."

"You don't have to. You're a good lawyer, and you want to get ahead. The Van Belden account is the perfect opportunity. I have no right to ask you to withdraw. I… Do you mind if I sit down?"

Now that the apology was over, she felt her legs giving way. And she needed her strength to go on. He gestured to one of the chairs. She practically fell into it. He sat in the other.

"I want you to understand," she went on.

He reached for her hands. "Clare, listen to me, you—"

She immediately withdrew from his clasp. She couldn't let him touch her yet.

"Please. Let me speak. Let me tell you why I found it so hard to trust you."

He pulled his hands back, but didn't draw away from her.

"I want you to know why I was so against office romances. It isn't just the principle—although there is that. It's because of something that happened to me."

She explained the circumstances that led to her being named partner, how she had constantly needed prove herself, watch her behavior and avoid any close attachments with lawyers. Of course, given what had happened in Boston, she was already wary.

As a recent law school graduate she had been fooled into believing that some blue-blooded colleague had been really interested in her, when all he wanted was access to her case files. Fortunately, she had learned the truth before any damage had been done, but she had promised herself it would never happen again. She had avoided relationships with coworkers and lawyers, perhaps even avoided relationships period. She had never allowed another man to come close to her. Not until Anton.

He moved forward. Without touching her, he imprisoned her, forcing her to look at him, to see the truth and the compassion in his blue eyes. "I'm sorry that happened to you, Clare. I'm sorry he hurt you. But you must know, I would never do that to you. You can trust me, Clare. You have to trust me. You—"

"I know."

"You know?" His voice was full of wonder as he reached for her, but she held back.

"I was going to tell you this, that day. I was going to lay my cards on the table and see what you felt. And I was going to suggest we go public. But Robert said you had been angling for the position since the beginning. I didn't even stop to think. It all came back to me. Everything that happened in Boston. I was so sure I was going through the same thing again."

"You didn't trust me?"

"Worse. I didn't trust myself. But I took it out on you and for that…" She took a deep breath and braced her shoulders as she looked him in the eye. "I am sorry."

"I've already accepted your apology, Clare. Not that you ever had to give it. Or to explain anything." He took both her hands into his. This time she let him. "I think I know how difficult this has been for you. How difficult it is for you to come today, to tell me all this. I want you to know how much it means to me. You came here, you demonstrated your trust. That's worth more than any apology."

His voice was rich and intense with feeling. His eyes filled with deep emotion. But before she could drown in them, he focused on some distant spot on the wall behind her.

"So now what?" he asked.

"That depends on you."

His chin jutted out. "I'm not going to withdraw my candidacy."

"I know that. Haven't you been listening?"

"I trust you to make the best decision possible based on merit."

"You do?"

"Yes, that's why I wouldn't, I couldn't withdraw. If you don't trust yourself about something like this, then nothing else between us is possible."

"Oh." Clare didn't know what she could say to

that. She studiously examined the patterns in the wooden floor.

"I want us to be something more, Clare, than just colleagues and good friends."

Clare lifted her face and saw such warmth and kindness, such passion in his eyes she thought she would melt. She leaned forward and kissed him, hesitantly at first, then more explosively.

Much later, seated on Anton's lap, his arms enfolding her, Clare said, "It's not going to be easy."

"No one said it would be. That's half the fun."

"I mean you work for me. That's courting disaster."

"At least you have courting on your mind!"

Clare tweaked him gently, which only got him laughing.

"I'll be menopausal in a couple of years."

"I'll be going through a midlife crisis."

"And I like being single. I like having my own hours and living in my own space. I don't know whether I can do this long-term thing." She buried her face in his shoulder. "I'm so afraid of losing you if I don't, and losing you if I do."

"You're not going to lose me, Clare," he said, wrapping her in his embrace. "We're just going to have to work hard at it, but on that score you have my complete trust."

"And you have mine," Clare said, and meant it.

CHAPTER 17

"I think that's it," Clare said to Lauren. "Do you want to say one last goodbye?"

"Yes. Give me a moment."

"We'll be out in the car, waiting," Clare said, squeezing her shoulder. "Take your time."

Lauren walked to the summit of the house and began her goodbye tour in Jeff's attic bedroom. Although his posters were long gone, the walls still bore their traces. Would the new owner see the patchwork pattern and speculate on who had lived here? Or would she paint immediately? Would she keep the wooden panels or toss them out?

Best not to know. Lauren headed down the staircase, her hand caressing the oak banister for the last time.

She stopped on the second floor, turning into Chrissie's bedroom, then into her master bedroom, where she looked out on the green lawn and the sprawling fruit trees. This had been "their" room. After Charles had left, she had never really settled into it, preferring to use her office during the day. Despite the bitter memories, she had to go through her adieus. She crossed the room, her steps echoing. She shut the wardrobe door for the last time. One minute later, she pulled the bedroom door behind her and headed down.

"Thank you, office," she said as she slowly paced her former work space. "I had some good times here. Some difficult ones, too." She stopped in the corner near the window where her desk had stood. With the toe of her shoe, she traced the floorboard, pausing on a familiar scratch. The rolling and swiveling of her chair had left its mark, imprinting her presence for as long as the wooden floor remained. Until then, the house would remember her.

"Goodbye, office." She walked towards the kitchen. The cupboards had been emptied. Some things didn't change: the kitchen tap was still dripping. She resisted the urge to give it one last twist and entered her favorite room.

Without the round wooden table, she didn't even recognize the breakfast room. This was not the place where she had come for comfort and tea, coffee and conversation. This was not her breakfast room. This was not her house. A house is not a home, and without her friends, her furniture, her memories, this was not her home. It was just another house on the block.

Lauren gently closed the front door. She glanced briefly at the porch where she and the children had spent many a late summer afternoon. Then she walked down the four front steps and out into the street.

* * *

"Are you okay?" Alice asked across the table at the Green Factory.

"I think so. It's hard to pack up twenty-four years of your life."

After dropping off the remaining boxes at the small apartment she would be renting temporarily, Clare and Lauren had joined Helen and Alice at their favorite restaurant. She had seen all of them separately since that eventful day at the studio, but this was the first time they had all been together.

They had each reported on their recent activities. Helen described Joe's apartment, where she would be staying until she found something for herself. She thought it too early to move in with him. Lauren could only commend the wise decision.

Clearly happy at having overcome a crisis in her marriage, Alice explained how Frank had begun to feel superfluous. The children had been such a central part of their relationship. With them gone, it had been difficult to forge a new foundation based on just the two of them. They had agreed to work hard at it, beginning with some marriage counseling sessions. They weren't going to get rid of the television, but Frank had promised to leave it off at least two nights a week and to set two other nights aside for rediscovering themselves. Everyone had ideas on what they could do together.

Then, Clare told about her latest victory: she had

convinced her partners to give a prestigious account to a young woman associate, setting her on the path to partnership.

Lauren was the last to talk about herself. Her friends gave her their full attention.

"No regrets?" Clare asked.

"No regrets," Lauren agreed with a warm smile for all of them. "Honestly, I feel like I have lost a house, but gained a life. Thank you."

She raised her glass to salute them and three other glasses came forward to produce a light clinking sound. Lauren drank her wine and put her glass down again. Tilting her head, she considered them.

"Well, maybe some regrets. Does it feel good to know that you were right, Clare?"

"Hell no! Besides, I wasn't right."

"Of course, you were. I should have sold the house much earlier and moved on to something else sooner."

"Maybe. But you weren't ready for it then. And at least this way, Charles doesn't get the house."

Lauren nodded. She wondered whether she had been spiteful to refuse Charles the sale, to wait for another, better offer. Probably. But sometimes a little revenge goes a long way. Her departure would never have been so smooth had she known Tracie and Charles would be inhabiting her former property.

"You know something, Lauren," Helen said. "I'm glad you didn't listen to Clare."

"Why's that?"

"I would never have found Joe," Helen replied with genuine sincerity.

"And I would never have pulled Frank away from the television and into marriage counseling."

"And I would never have decided to try something with Anton."

Feeling very much like Dorothy as she prepared to click her red slippers and return to Kansas, Lauren looked at her friends and laughed. They were back where they started—a divorced writer, a workaholic lawyer, a married accountant, and a semiattached computer whiz, but they were also older, wiser and a great deal happier. They had come to terms with love, explored their minds and hearts and learned to trust themselves and each other.

"So now what, Lauren?" Alice asked.

"Well, I move into my new place." She dipped the delicious bread into the spicy sauce.

"You're not going to visit Chrissie?" Helen asked.

"No. Not now."

The question had come up, of course. When the sale of the house had gone through, Chrissie had suggested her mother join her in Vienna for a short visit. Lauren had been tempted, but decided against it. It was time for her to begin her new life, and time to let her daughter get on with her own.

"Maybe next year."

She popped the bread into her mouth. She couldn't resist licking her fingers.

"So you move into your new place and…" Clare prompted her.

"I work on my book. Michael thinks I don't have much revising to do."

Clare, Alice and Helen exchanged knowing glances. "Michael, huh?"

"Yes. Michael." She pretended not to notice the silent gloating. "Nothing serious. I'm too happy with the single life to think of anything else. Which reminds me." Lauren reached for more bread. "He tells me *Modern Times* is looking for someone to write about life with a motorcycle gang. Anyone interested in hitting the road with me?"

Clare opened her mouth to speak, Helen raised her hand to volunteer, Alice and Lauren's eyes met and they all laughed.

* * * * *

There comes a time in every woman's life when she needs more.

Sometimes finding what you want means leaving everything you love. Big-hearted, warm and funny, Flying Lessons is a story of love and courage as Beth Holt Martin sets out to change her life and her marriage, for better or for worse.

Flying Lessons

by

Peggy Webb

Available May 2006
TheNextNovel.com

REQUEST YOUR FREE BOOKS!

2 FREE NOVELS TO INTRODUCE YOU TO OUR BRAND-NEW LINE!

Next™

There's the life you planned. And there's what comes next.

There are things inside us
we don't know how to express,
but that doesn't mean
they're not there.

A poignant story about a woman
coming to terms with her relationship
with her father and learning to open up
to the other men in her life.

The Birdman's Daughter

by Cindi Myers

HARLEQUIN®
Next™

Available April 2006
TheNextNovel.com

HN38

You're never too old to sneak out at night

BJ thinks her younger sister, Iris, needs a love interest. So she does what any mature woman would do and organizes an Over-Fifty Singles Night. When her matchmaking backfires it turns out to be the best thing either of them could have hoped for.

Over 50's Singles Night

by Ellyn Bache

Available April 2006
TheNextNovel.com

HN37

A Boca Babe on a Harley?

Harriet's former life as a Boca Babe—where only looks, money and a husband count—left her struggling for freedom. Finally gaining control of her path, she's leaving that life behind as she takes off on her Harley. When she drives straight into a mystery that is connected to her past, will she be able to stay true to her future?

Dirty Harriet

by Miriam Auerbach

HN40

Available April 2006
TheNextNovel.com

Life is full of hope.

Facing a family crisis, Melinda and
her husband are forced to look
at their lives and end up learning
what is really important.

Falling Out
of Bed

by
Mary Schramski

HARLEQUIN®
Next™

Available May 2006
TheNextNovel.com

HN41

It's a dating jungle out there!

Four thirtysomething women with a fear of dating form a network of support to empower each other as they face the trials and travails of modern matchmaking in Los Angeles.

The I Hate To Date Club

by
Elda Minger